CROSS MY PALM

The Fortunes of Grace Hammer
(first published as *Hammer*)

Cross My Palm

Sara Stockbridge

Chatto & Windus
LONDON

Published by Chatto & Windus 2011

2 4 6 8 10 9 7 5 3 1

Copyright © Sara Stockbridge 2011

Sara Stockbridge has asserted her right under the Copyright, Designs
and Patents Act 1988 to be identified as the author of this work.

First published in Great Britain in 2011 by
Chatto & Windus
Random House, 20 Vauxhall Bridge Road,
London SW1V 2SA

www.randomhouse.co.uk

Addresses for companies within The Random House Group Limited
can be found at: www.randomhouse.co.uk/offices.htm

The Random House Group Limited Reg. No. 954009

Palmistry map of the hand © *Illustrated London News*
Ltd/Mary Evans Picture Library

A CIP catalogue record for this book
is available from the British Library

ISBN 9780701185046

The Random House Group Limited supports The Forest Stewardship Council®
(FSC®), the leading international forest certification organisation.
All our titles that are printed on Greenpeace approved FSC® certified paper carry
the FSC® logo. Our paper procurement policy can be found at
www.randomhouse.co.uk/environment

Typeset by Palimpsest Book Production Ltd, Falkirk, Stirlingshire
Printed and bound in Great Britain by
CPI Mackays, Chatham ME5 8TD

For Cobalt

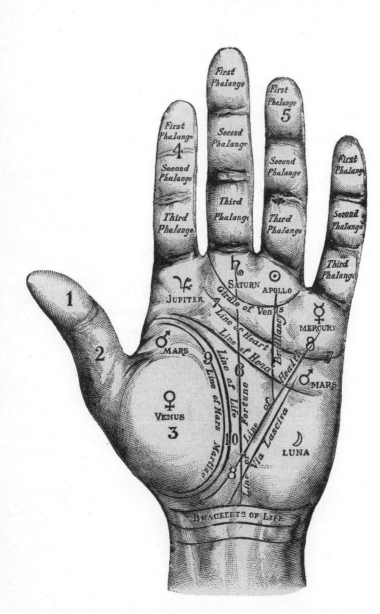

A palmistry map of the hand c.1890, from *Illustrated London News*

My mother said, I never should
Play with the gypsies in the wood.
If I did she would say,
'Naughty girl to disobey.'
Your hair shan't curl and your shoes won't shine,
Gypsy girl, you shan't be mine.
And my father said that if I did
He'd rap my head with the teapot lid.
The wood was dark, the grass was green,
Along came Sally with a tambourine.
I went to sea, no ship to get across,
I paid ten shillings for a blind white horse.
I was up on his back and off in a crack,
Sally, tell my mother that I shan't come back.

Anon

Chapter One

Rose

Who knows where we came from? You may guess yourself blue in the face if it matters to you. Let us say I was born in a painted wagon, with golden coins in my black gypsy hair, if you like. Let us say my mother wove magic and my father was a proud duke of Egypt. Of Egypt? you say – being an inquisitive sort. How came he from Egypt? Of all the places in the wide world! Well, my dear, that is what the Romani men call themselves. Princes of Egypt. Who knows whether they sprang from the Egyptian desert dust, or fell from the sky? Who knows indeed? These things are a mystery, lost in ancient time. And that is all you need to know. A deep, dark stare will stop you there. Feeling, perhaps, that you have strayed into discourteous territory and must wind your green neck in, you will offer me your hand. And so it is your secrets we shall see, in just another moment, after I have finished looking at your face, holding you still, until you squirm in your seat, just a little. And then I will flash the gold in my teeth at you, and ask you to cross my palm with silver.

Let me tell you your own heart. Your fortune, your destiny.

How do I know? It is written on the flat of your hand, for anyone who can read it to see.

*

When I was a young thing I would study my own hand, for hours, under the optical glass. It is on the end of my own arm, after all, and I must carry it about all day long. I would search my palm for lucky stars, husbands, children. The hand changes, little by little, every day, like creeping sand. Of course it does! If your fortune was set in stone what purpose would there be in rising, and dressing, eating, speaking, moving from here to there? Romani do not have their fortunes read, especially not the men, for life is like streaky bacon, they say: there is some fat, and then some lean, and you had better take them together.

So what does my own hand say? It tells me that I shall be rich enough – some time this year. That I shall never be married. That my heart is strong, my honesty doubtful. And that I shall surely suffer death by drowning. Well, I have an easy enough answer to that. I avoid boats. And deep baths. And I never cross the river. I hope it will disappear, that little star on the palm of my left hand, on the Mount of the Moon. But I don't care to look often.

On my left hand is drawn the map of my forebears, my foundation, the bricks that are laid; on my right, the weather, the changes, the path I have made, down to the very last detail of tomorrow, written in creases that cross the line of Fate – which runs from the wrist to the Saturn finger, through the very centre of the palm. (Avoid the person who has no Fate line. They lack interest and direction, and may sap the spirit.) If I look hard enough, it seems I can read the address at which I must keep my appointment this evening. Twenty-seven, Cavendish Square, it says. And there, in tiny criss-cross lines, the time and date: eight o'clock, the thirtieth of May, 1860.

*

Lady Quayle's curtains are drawn across but aristocratic laughter peals upon the evening air as I ring the bell. The maid admits me on sight, though I have never called here before. Through the hall she ushers me, down the corridor, and throwing open the grand door of the dining room, she announces me, as all the women fall silent at the table.

'My lady, Miss Lee is here.'

A Mrs Radish comes first – the maid announces her. She approaches the table as if she were hoping I might bite her. Small, uncertain fingers I see, as she crosses my palm with a sixpence, and more rouge than is decent on her withering cheeks. Her hands are too soft, and curled up, like a squirrel's. I know her first question before she asks it. And not because I can read her mind but because it may as well be tattooed on her forehead.

'Can you tell me, Miss Lee,' she ventures, 'do you see a good match, perchance, for my daughter?'

'Well, indeed, Mrs Radish, perhaps I had better look at your daughter's hand to tell you that.'

'Oh,' she says. 'I see. Of course.' The girlish ringlets in her

3

hair quiver as she wonders how to approach the matter another way. Her hand twitches in mine, feebly.

'If it would interest you, Mrs Radish, I might tell you something instead about your own fortune – your standing, perhaps, in the future. In the way of society, say.'

'Oh!' she says. 'Yes.'

'The Vital and Saturnian lines together reveal the prospects for your health and comfort in the years to come – material, social, financial.'

'Do tell.' Now she looks lively enough.

I show Mrs Radish how clean her hand is of feathered lines, islands, chains, denoting a life free of worry and responsibility. She's pleased with that. No crosses (they signify obstacles) on the leading lines. Now she makes a little grunt of satisfaction. She has a short Cerebral line, which marks a weak will and a lack of conscience: a person who is happy enough to leave her arrangements to somebody else. I do not mention this, or the grille on her Apollo mount, which shows she's too vain to take my advice anyhow. Finally I show her her own frail but relentless Life line, which runs all the way to eighty-three, or -four – if she takes enough fresh air and rest, and avoids tomato. And while I am telling her all this I am pitying her poor daughter, who will never escape this burden, not until she is getting old herself, and threadbare.

Next, a blowzy, curly-haired pudding, ushered forth by the company, protesting all the way. I do not catch her name above the squeaks and exclamations that come in with her. Once the door has closed she settles herself into the chair and thrusts out her lily-white hand. Greedy girl, with her lace cuffs, and her fat red face. We look at one another across the tablecloth. She blushes a little.

'You must cross my palm with silver first, my pretty miss,' I tell her. Of course she hasn't thought of that, being the sort of girl who gets along just dandy without carrying any money, and must exit the room to borrow a suitable coin. Upon returning she dumps a threepenny bit on the table, rather huffily, as if she had been cheated out of it. I don't trouble to tell her I have been paid already, handsomely indeed. I make her take the threepenny bit up again and cross my palm in the proper manner. A silver coin, to mark the sign of the cross, it wards off the devil himself, my dear. You wouldn't want him to sit in on our little conference, would you? Now then. What have we here?

An uncommonly large hand for a lady. The palm, that is. If she had been a poor girl she might have put her practical talents to good use, but as she is not, of course, it is soft and flabby, a great idle plate of pork fat. She smiles prettily, as if it will help her fortune along. Well. It is already written in your hand, dear. And, as anyone can see, you don't do much of anything but eat and lounge about so it is safe to call it fixed there. 'You will marry a kind man with an adequate fortune,' I tell her. She frowns at that. 'I see one child, a daughter.' (Who will be fat also.) 'You will receive a dinner invitation shortly. You must accept it.' Her hand lies on mine, like a sandbag or a dead thing on a slab.

'And you must avoid too much invigoration or you may suffer seizures of the heart, around the age of thirty-six.'

5

So they follow, with their various fortunes. I talk of matters they imagine no one else could know, I lay their secrets on the tabletop, their own private wishes, things they have not admitted to themselves; I watch them gasp, and shrink a little, and shake their heads, forget themselves, as if they were alone; and then they look up from the cloth at me, as though lost, and I tell them the future.

You will find your true love over the seas. You, you will live to be old, and die happy, in a soft bed. Beware a man with a missing finger. A man in a tall grey hat. Beware the letter R. The month of May. Oak trees in the rain. Tottenham Court Road.

All true.

But one thing I keep to myself. I see it in the last hand of the evening's procession.

Her name is Emily. She is a plain thing, dressed in drab flannel, with her hair coiled in two buns above her ears. She enters the room like a little grey mouse, peeping around the door before she steps in, and I suppose for a moment she is a servant, come to tell me that the ladies are done. But then she sits.

'Good evening,' she says politely. She keeps her little mouse paws in her lap.

'Good evening to you, miss,' I say. She seems happy enough. I cannot imagine that she would want to ask me anything, sat so serene in the chair. 'Have they pressed you to come in?'

'No, indeed not.'

'Good enough. Then are you wanting to keep your hands to yourself?'

'I am not,' she says. 'But . . . perhaps . . . I am reluctant.'

'How so?'

'I am not sure it is a good idea,' says she, 'to discover one's fortune.'

Now, reluctance to show the palms of one's hands is the sign of someone with a dark secret to keep – but a person who sits down in the chair, of their own free will, only to fold their hands under the table is a conundrum indeed.

'I see,' I say, though I do not. 'So why are you here?'

'I am curious,' says Emily. 'Only I suppose that I am seeking some assurance, before we begin, that it is the right thing to do.'

'I don't give assurances,' I tell her. 'I only read hands.'

'Yes.' She looks down at them, clenched together. Indeed, I am curious myself – enough to reach across and seize her by the wrists! But I wait, as Emily makes up her mind. All of a sudden she thrusts her hand into her pocket and pulls out a half-crown. She holds it up in the lamplight, glinting silver. And as I uncurl my palm upon the table and she crosses it, it seems we are stirring up evil things.

Emily's hands are small and pale. She presents them a little closed, as if she could not hold them flat, with her fingers held tight together and I know, sure enough, she is keeping a secret. Anyone could tell you that. Square palms, tapered fingertips, a practical, yet sensitive hand. Her index and ring fingers match in length, indicating a balanced temperament. Thumbs, low-set, steadying the ethereal fingertips. Her Vital line is delicate but unbroken, her Cerebral line straight, revealing, in combination with the long first phalange of the thumb, a firm will and a clear head. Emily might look timid alright but she is tough enough, strong and hardworking. The Mensal line is even, showing a faithful heart – free of islands or forks, but for a red point below the Mount of Apollo. Passion, it says, hidden desires. Or angina. It could be that here is the key to her secret.

It is curiously hard to read, Emily's palm. Simple, yet impenetrable. No stars, no feathers, not a square anywhere.

'No squares. What does that mean?'

'We look for squares on the reckless hand, my dear. They offer protection. You can get by without them.'

'And stars?'

'Stars! They can be a blessing or a curse. They signal momentous events.'

'No stars?'

'Stars are rare.'

'A quiet life then.' She says it with a little sigh, as if that was all she came to hear.

'A quiet life, my dear.'

I fold up her hand and let it go.

Only I lie. I never tell her about the cross. The little cross on the Saturnian line, at its end, the grille upon the Mount of Mars, the Cerebral line sloping to the Rascette where it terminates in another little cross that matches the first. All there, on the same palm, clear as print.

Death, they say. *Fearful, violent death.*

*

The ladies are taking coffee as I come out, chattering, but quietly, as if they are sharing urgent secrets. They fall silent

8

as I pass through the room, eyes fixing on me – as I pause at the door to bid them goodnight – lapping up exotic waves of gypsy mystery, perhaps hoping for sparks to shoot from my mouth, or some other parting flourish. As the salon door closes behind me I hear the babble boiling up again, giggling, whispering.

Lady Quayle herself sees me out. 'Thank you, my dear. It has been a most amusing evening. Shall I contact you at the same address in future?' Then she laughs at her own question, a little laugh like a silver bell tinkling. 'The future! Oh! What I mean to say is, not *shall* but—'

'I know what you meant to say, Lady Quayle. And yes, indeed, you may leave me a message at the same address.'

*

The Buttered Bun Coffee House, 14 Soho Square
Proprietress: Mrs R. Bunion
Open every day from 8 o'clock, hot breakfasts served, best
  bacon
Tea, or coffee, two slices and an egg, 3d

Lady Quayle sends her footman to the Buttered Bun not a week later, on a Tuesday afternoon. Mrs Bunion calls up, asking if I am in – 'There's a footman here,' she tells me, 'rather a pompous fellow, all in yellow, like a great stuffed lemon. He's brought a letter – scented, if you please.'

I decide I am in, and down I go to have a look at him. His uniform fairly lights up the shop. He withers me at ten paces, holding out the envelope with the very tips of his gloved fingers.

As curt as he can manage, he tells me he has instructions to wait while I read it. It smells of lily-of-the-valley, and this is what it says:

My dear Miss Lee,
    I hope my letter finds you in good health. I must confess I am thrown into something of a turmoil this morning – with the unfolding of an event I am sure you will recall predicting only last week, at our mystic soirée. I shall say no more here other than that I have received an unexpected caller, bearing very bad news. Naturally I am keen to consult you again, as soon as is possible. I hope you will accommodate me, privately this time, at your earliest convenience.
    Yours sincerely,
    Lady M. Quayle

Now let me see. It is possible I might very dimly recall predicting some such thing, if I were to try hard enough. Every one of my clients imagines I must remember each tiny detail of their precious fortunes, as if I cared for every twist and turn of them. Of course I will go to Lady Quayle again – she does seem all-a-fluster. But she will like my advice all the better if she has to wait for it. I send the footman back empty-handed.

And I leave the matter unattended. That day, the next day and the next. On Friday I send a note back. It smells of lavender and this is what it says:

My dear Lady Quayle,

I hope you have not suffered too much waiting. Time, indeed, outruns us all. At last I find myself at liberty to attend you. Only name the day.

Miss Rose Lee

Friday midday the note drops through her letterbox and Friday afternoon the footman comes back, his furious yellow uniform not a day older than before. He fixes his eye on the middle distance while I read the message.

Dear Miss Lee,

I pray you will be able to give me the benefit of your wisdom this very afternoon. Perhaps you might return with my footman. I shall be more than ready to receive you.

Yours most sincerely,

Lady M. Quayle

Well, I am not about to return with the footman. He can suffer the humiliations his yellow felt suit attracts in Soho Square all by himself and good luck to him. Besides, it won't hurt to wind our lady's spring a little tighter.

I go to her at six, just as the dark is coming down on Cavendish Square. She is looking out as I arrive, a step back from the window. The curtain drops abruptly as I ring the bell. The maid admits me.

My lady is at leisure in the drawing room, arranged informally across a velvet armchair, but stiff as if her joints had rusted. She greets me with a little exclamation, eyebrows jumping – she'd forgotten I was coming, how delightful. She calls for coffee, makes polite conversation while we wait for it to be brought up by the butler. He has barely set the tray down before she shoos him away. Only when she has finished pouring and tinkering and fussed the sugar lumps into our cups does she look me in the eye. And then she almost flushes, pink with shame. Her head tilts a little downwards so that she seems to look up at me. I could squash her under my thumb. I say nothing at all.

After a moment she says, 'I must confess, Miss Lee, that last week, when I procured your services for the benefit of my guests, perhaps . . . perhaps I was not altogether . . . Perhaps my intentions were not altogether serious.' Now Lady Quayle bites her lip. She seems to be struggling: in fact, she seems rather unsure of what it is that she wants to say.

'Your intentions are really your own business, my lady,' I say, hoping to help her along.

'What I mean,' she says suddenly, quite decisively, 'what I mean to say is that I came to the whole business – having my fortune read, that is, and those of my party – from a rather discourteous . . . no, indeed, from a *disrespectful* standpoint. I am sorry to admit that I brought you here that evening for the entertainment of my guests. And, indeed, although I cannot speak for them, I myself took the view that there was really nothing in it at all.' Here she stops and looks at me with wide, sorry eyes. Eyes that might repent any one of the seven deadly sins.

Well! How to tell her? Politely, I mean. Is this really what I've crossed London Town for? But of course not. She wants another reading: clutching and rubbing her palms together, twisting her French lace handkerchief around her restless fingers.

'Well,' I tell her, 'I thank you for your kind and frank concern, my lady. But to be frank in return, it is really all the same to me as long as I am paid for my trouble.'

'Oh,' she says. It hasn't occurred to Lady Quayle before that I shall get along quite happily without her endorsement.

'I must impress upon you, my lady, that there is no need for upset or apology on this score. You are entitled to your own opinion after all! Along with the rest of humanity. And I bear you not the slightest ill will on account of it. No one, indeed, is obliged to have their palm read.' And with these words I drain my cup and get up to take my leave.

'Wait!' she says. The word hangs in the air in its own small bubble of panic. She is holding my arm. She takes her hand away. 'Please, Miss Rose,' she says. 'You misunderstand me.'

'How so, my lady?'

'I thought last week that there was nothing in it,' she says, 'but now my mind has been quite changed. Turned quite around, you see.'

I sit back down again.

'Do you remember?' she asks me. The answer to this is always the same: no, I do not remember. 'You told me that I should receive an unexpected caller. You said they would arrive without announcement and bring news that may be troubling . . .' Now she says it, a small bell does ring in some dusty corner of my head. 'Well,' she says, 'on Tuesday morning I was preparing to ride out to Kew, for a meeting of the Surrey Ladies Charitable Committee, and then to take a little country air and a turn around the Palm House, and was just remarking to myself before the glass, as I fastened my hat, that this may be the day the unexpected caller comes – as you had said they were to come in the very near future – and that if it was to be today then what a pity that would be as I would be out when they called . . . when the front doorbell rang. Well! No one was expected. No one at all. Unless it was a tradesman come to the wrong entrance, and how very unlikely would that be? And so I left my dressing room and stood at the top of the stairs while the footman answered the door.' Having gone all around the houses to come to the point Lady Quayle pauses dramatically – as if the mystery caller needed any more of a drum roll. 'And there,' she says, 'on the doorstep, was no one other than my daughter, Tabitha.'

Another pause – long enough that you might have driven an omnibus through it – as I wonder why you mayn't be expecting a family member at your own door.

Lady Quayle notices my bewilderment. 'Now, one's own daughter mightn't seem to be an unexpected caller, Miss Rose, but that she was supposed to be in Wiltshire, at the grand house of the Dent family – she is engaged to be married into the family, you see, to their fine young son George, Twelfth Earl of Leland – and a very good family it is, very good indeed. At any rate, she was intended to stay until next week, acquainting herself with his sisters, taking an enthu-siastic part in the family's rural pursuits, and so forth. And there she was on the doorstep – *arriving quite without announcement*, just as you said. Well, I wondered what on earth had happened for her to be there, pouting and scowling at the footman.' At this there is a knock on the door – I am hoping it will be this Tabitha girl, who has caused her poor mother such an upset, but it is the butler, come to tell her that Lord Quayle will dine at his club that evening. Lady Quayle waits while he delivers his message, looking for all the world as if she has never heard of Lord Quayle and has no interest at all in his dining arrangements, or comment to make regarding them.

'Thank you, Thomas,' is all she has to say about it.

Once Thomas has left the room, I fancy he stands at the other side of the door with his ear to it. My lady sips at her coffee, distracted, sets the cup down. 'Where were we?' she says, 'Oh, yes. And now for the worst part. Tabitha did indeed bring troubling news. "The engagement," she says, "*is all off.*" Those were her very words. "The engagement is all off!" As if it were a cricket match! And then she flounced up to her rooms, where she has taken most of her meals since. I have pressed her on the matter, of course, but she will say nothing more about it.' She sits back in her chair as if to say, Well! And what do you think of that?

I believe I disappoint her. I can find nothing at all to think about any of it — nothing I might say out loud, at any rate. She searches my face for something she is evidently missing and then, giving up on it, cuts to the chase.

'So I wanted to ask you, Miss Rose, to have another look. At my hand.'

'Very well, Lady Quayle. And what am I to look for?'

'Oh! Well, what is to come of all this, I suppose.'

'I can only tell my lady her own fortune from her own hand.'

'Yes, I see.' She stops, with her palm up, halfway across the table, and her mouth a little open, as if to catch a fly. Then she looks up at the ceiling, up to where Miss Tabitha sulks and languishes in her room. Perhaps she considers fetching her down to have her palm read, and thinks better of it. Then she thrusts her hand the last inch across the cloth. 'Look for omens, Miss Rose. Good or bad. And tell me how I am to proceed.'

The second time I look at Lady Quayle's hand I remember. For it's all there, plain as day. I'm not making it up after all. I tell her that no clear way forward presents itself, and that no decision or journey must be undertaken until after the new moon. 'Next Friday, that would be, my lady.'

Only this time I look at her left hand as well.

'Oh,' she says, peering at it as if she could read it also. 'What does the left hand tell one?'

The left hand is the hand of fixed fate, the fortune you are born with. The hand of your inheritance and constitution. But that doesn't sound much of a thrill. So I say, 'The left hand, my lady, refers to the hidden side of the character – indeed, the very soul. It can reveal the darker secrets of the heart, the fortunes bound up with desire, buried thought, forgotten treasures.'

She looks a little nervous. 'Goodness,' she says.

There is nothing much at all on my lady's left hand. Indeed, I don't believe I have ever seen such a blank palm. And soft, too, unresisting. Like a wet piece of sponge cake.

'Well, my lady,' I say, 'the clarity of this palm denotes a generous, selfless nature.'

'Oh,' she says.

'A person of good faith and upright morals.'

'Well,' she says, 'I do endeavour to attend church on Sunday mornings, if breakfast is done in good time.'

Good enough Vital line, a wisp of a Mensal, no Saturnian

to speak of. 'The fine heart line,' I tell her, 'reveals your charitable endeavours, in spite of your modest nature . . .'

'Indeed,' she says, 'I must confess, my charitable activities do keep me very busy.'

And barely there, a faint Cerebral line, to match the other – wispy and fractured as the thoughts in her sweet head. Lady Quayle is the type whose trust might easily be taken advantage of. And so I tell her, as politely as I can, 'Your good nature may be your downfall, my lady.'

'My downfall?' she says. 'When?'

'Please, Lady Quayle, do not alarm yourself. I am simply noting the obstacles that may lie in the path of a generous and trusting nature such as yours. I can see no impending doom. Only you must be careful.'

'Careful?'

'Of . . . taking others too much into your confidence, let us say. And confidence tricksters.'

'Well!' she says, looking much relieved. 'And when am I ever to come across any of those?'

'Oh, and another thing, my lady. Avoid the colour yellow.'

'Yellow? What a pity,' she says. 'I like yellow.'

*

That evening I head to the Haymarket, that thoroughfare of lively entertainments and a thousand likely women, so celebrated every day of late in stiff letters to *The Times*. I find my dear friend Miss Lillie Daley in the foyer of the Theatre Royal, in a ravishing black-and-white-striped silk gown, with a red rosette at her throat.

'You look a proper treat, my dear,' I tell her. 'Have you dined yet?'

'I have not,' she says.

'I've a fancy for a good pork chop.'

'To the Albany then.'

We make our way up towards Regent Circus, the evening crowd churning all around us, laughing and carousing, the smart tarts rustling in silk, bubbling with champagne, batting their eyelashes at the gentlemen, leaning forward to give them an eyeful; shouts for tables, more oysters, more fizz. Ducking out of the crush we cut down Jermyn Street and come out on Piccadilly: grand and wide, shining with lights, stretching down past the great mansion houses all the way to Hyde Park Corner and Apsley House, the very grandest of them all. The toffs only have to follow their noses up the hill to the tarts, you see.

At the Albany we order pork chops and a good rare steak. 'How's tricks, my dear?' I ask her, once the wine is served.

'Good enough,' says she. 'And how's the fortune game?'

'Funny you should ask,' I tell her, 'for I have met a most interesting new client.'

'Oh?'

'Just very recently. A local lady. And very nicely placed she is too.'

A lady (of the Haymarket variety) at the next table leans her head a little over our way. The ostrich feather bounces on her hat, as if it was giving us the wink.

'Nicely placed, eh? Is that so?' says Lillie, giving her daggers. Ostrich Hat looks as if she might say something, but decides against it. She takes her feather out of our conversation and pops another oyster in her beak.

'Very nicely placed indeed. And a charitable soul, too,' I tell Lillie, when I have her attention again. 'Which brought me to thinking – mayn't you like to be reformed once more? Any time soon.'

'Well, Gypsy Miss! You mean give over this life of vice and take the straight and narrow path to salvation?'

'Doesn't it sound like a good idea?'

'I could give it another whirl.'

After dinner is done we fetch up to Windmill Street, to have a glass or two at the infamous Argyll Rooms, which have been causing such a fluster among polite society lately – at least, among the women, who never go. The gas jets light up the night inside, burning high above the heads of the crowd, up above the dance-floor. The band is playing The Shanghai Polka as we walk in. We take tickets up to the gallery, and a glass of plain gin. Lillie waves to Kate Hamilton, wicked witch, once the reigning beauty of the Haymarket girls, who wears a moustache on her florid face nowadays. She is standing at the entrance to the private alcove. Some of her girls are leaning over the balcony, drinking champagne from Venetian goblets. She beckons Lillie over with a thick red finger, diamonds flashing at us in the gaslight.

'We'll have to go over for a minute,' says Lillie.

'You will,' I tell her. 'I'm not speaking to it.'

'Damn you.'

Off she goes to greet the fat finger. I sip my gin and look down at the throng, swirling in satin and rouge and finest French kid, on their express route to the devil himself. And a pretty picture they are too. I sup my gin and look idly over to the counter, wondering how long Lillie will be detained by Lady Hamilton and if she will be forced to have a glass of sham. And all of a sudden my eye is caught by a little face. It is a face quite out of place in this fancy hall, like a pebble in a jeweller's window, a serious, plain little face, and I know it instantly.

It is Emily. Emily the mouse, who has square palms and ethereal fingertips, a little red point beneath her Apollo finger. And fearful, violent death marked on her tiny paw.

Whatever is she doing here, with her hair in those same buns and still the same plain grey flannel dress? She can't be working the balcony, not dressed like that and not with Lady Hamilton just across the gallery, but she doesn't look to be enjoying herself either. She's sat all alone, with her hands in her lap and her face as blank as a clean slate. It's as if she just dropped out of the sky smack into the Argyll Rooms, by mistake, and doesn't know where she is. Or as if she's not really there at all – nobody else seems to notice her. I realize I am staring and turn my attention to my glass.

Surely she can't be on her own. And she isn't. Here come her companions. A man, young enough and handsome, dark, bearing champagne, and a young lady, with delicately flushed cheeks and golden hair, a fair complexion, like a china doll, smiling brightly at her friend, flushed with excitement. For sure the fellow has taken her for a turn around the dance-floor. The Haymarket ladies look her up and down, in her pale pink satin and pearls – so much the opposite of their flash and brash finery. Who does she think she is? And what might she be doing at the Argyll Rooms, where her father or uncle might go but her sister or mother will never set foot? Sightseeing, that's what. They have seen her sort before. They sneer and flick cigarette ash at the back of her dress.

The three toast each other and drink. The pink satin doll leans into her beau, giggling. As she tosses her golden ringlets and turns to look over the balustrade, I see him glance at Emily, the look in his eyes as they meet hers. And then I see him, the cad. I see him slip his hand down under the table and take Emily's little mouse paw. Seize it, in a strong hand, interlocking her fingers with his, pushing between them, pressing her neat white hand backwards into her lap as if he were pressing himself between her legs. She doesn't resist, though she starts and makes wide eyes at him, but her friend is oblivious, looking over the dance-floor, cooing at the swirling throng below. And then he reaches down and pulls up the hem of Emily's skirt, inching it up to her knee, and slides his hand up under it. She makes a little shudder, closes her eyes and leans her head back, just a whisker.

'I've got away at last,' says Lillie, behind me, making me jump. 'Fancy another gin?'

The handsome cad has taken his hand back. Emily smoothes her skirts under the table and flicks her eyes around the room. I do not want her to see me: something like a panic grips the back of my neck.

'Let's go on to the Holborn, shall we, dear? Or Coney's,' I say.

'If you like.' She looks at my taut face. 'Seen a ghost, have you?'

Violent death. In the words of my grandmother, *fearful, violent death.*

It's not a sign that pops up every day. And, having seen that mousey creature at the Argyll rooms, out on the town with the swirl of Piccadilly all around her – I find her haunting my thoughts: her small serious face, and her flannel dress, and then the palm of that timid hand, and I begin to wonder about that fearful, violent death. Poor Emily! Would she be crushed beneath the wheels of a cab? Trampled by horses? Robbed and beaten in a dark alleyway, set on by some dreadful fiend? Garrotted? Shot? Was she to fall from a high window? On to railings? To suffer knotted guts – most heinous agony, I have heard, and can come on suddenly, without warning – or to choke on a piece of sausage, perhaps? All these death throes poor Emily suffers in succession, wheezing and clawing and staggering before my mind's eye. Then she stops, and I, too, for a rest. And then comes the thought I have been pushing away.

Poor Emily's horrid and deliberate murder. Or, rather, murders. I watch her play them out: a cut throat, a knife through the heart, a strangling, a smothering, a drop of poison. It was seeing her there, holding hands under the table with that rogue's ladylove gazing gaily out across the dance-floor. Little Emily Mouse, caught in the swirling tangle of the Argyll Rooms, keeping such company . . . An uncomfortable notion slides its sinister fingers around my stomach. A feeling more than a suspicion.

I shake my head to revive her. It may never happen at all!

Just because I've seen Miss Mouse out on the town among the tarts and swells there's no reason to suppose she's getting herself into trouble. Lines can change, I tell myself, and so they do. The actions we take every day alter the course of our lives and the fortune that is written on the palms of our hands.

If it were not true, what purpose would there be in rising and dressing, moving from here to there?

Chapter Two

Rose

The following week Lady Quayle's footman is back again, and thoroughly ticked off about it. If I was in the habit of reading my own palm I would have seen him coming, in his stiff blue uniform, swearing under his breath at the tarts in Soho Square. I tell him he looks well in his new suit. He sneers, handsomely.

It seems that Lady Quayle has taken to the gypsy fashion, for inside her letter was a sprig of lavender.

Dear Rose,

    I must consult you once again. Might we say this evening? I hope you will receive this message in good time. I shall wait for you in any case.

    Yours,

    Lady M. Quayle

Well! What matter could my poor lady have pressing so urgently upon her? What curiosity could be burning such a hole in her head? I imagine her pacing back and forth before the window, wringing her fine lace handkerchief. This time I make the cheery footman wait while I scribble a short reply –

Dear Lady Quayle,
    I do regret I am quite unable to attend you at any civil hour this evening. However, I shall pass by at eleven. If you can receive me, leave a light burning before the window.
        Until then, sincerely,
        Rose

– and hand it to the footman, who is sneering at me still.

'I have sealed it with a curse,' I tell him. 'In the absence of wax.' He snorts as if to say he couldn't give tuppence for gypsy curses. But I know he won't read it all the same.

*

I don't go in for con tricks, not usually. My grandmother never did. She was rich just from the women who'd come to the camp to have their fortunes told by the famous Hannah Smith. She read palms, and tea-leaves, and cards – she was never seen without a pack of cards in her hand. And though people believed every word she said, she never took advantage of it, even though they were *gadje* and a lot of us would have said they were fair game. I expect she would be quite angry at some of my capers. But, then, Lillie and I have to survive on our own, by our wits, with only each other to count on.

There are those who can give you a good enough reading, but at the end of it they'll 'see' something bad, a curse, perhaps, that they'll lift for twenty pounds, or a jinxed inheritance that you'll have to bury at the cemetery, every last penny of it, to cleanse it of evil. Well, of course, you'll never see it again. These are common tricks, and vulgar. I like a trick to have a little more of a game about it, give the mark a chance to work it out – to win, if you like – not just grab their money and run. I'd call that plain thieving.

It's true enough that Lillie and I always pick someone who isn't too sharp – we don't do it often for the right mark doesn't happen along every day – and perhaps it'd be fair enough to say they haven't the wit to give them a decent chance against us but that's their own funeral. If they woke themselves up a bit they might be very much more careful of putting such trust in the hands of a stranger.

*

At eleven the light is there in the window, threatening to set the curtains on fire. And there is Lady Quayle, looking down over the street with no attempt this time to disguise it. She lets me in herself, gingerly, signalling to me to make no noise, and ushers me up the stairs, to her private dressing room. His Lordship is due back earlier than expected, says she, and he will take a very dim view of our activities. He regards this sort of thing as utter tosh, she tells me. (And who can blame him.) But he won't disturb us in here.

Lady Quayle's private dressing room is much smaller than the parlour. But, then, I was brought up in a painted wagon, and feel quite at home in a smaller room. We settle ourselves across a small table in the corner, screened from the door, the candlelight guttering on our faces. I notice she is carrying a rabbit's foot.

I am expecting my lady to thrust her palm at me in her usual fashion, but she surprises me. She leans over the cloth as if to whisper in my ear.

'Well, Miss Rose,' she says, 'I have spoken to Tabitha, yesterday, about this dreadful business. She would not entertain it at first, but by and by I persuaded her to talk of it a little.' I imagine the good lady wheedling her impetuous daughter, following her from room to room, grinding down her patience. 'The situation,' she tells me gravely, 'is very much worse than I previously thought.' I open my mouth to ask her how so, but she charges on. 'When she took leave of the Dent family home in such an unseemly hurry I assumed that one of the Dent men had made an improper advance, or that young George had made overtures to another girl, or some such thing. But now I find the reason is very much worse – and, indeed, quite impassable, as Tabitha flatly refuses to see sense.'

Now, nothing could be worse, among the Roma, than men making 'improper advances' towards one's own daughters. And after that, nothing could be worse than breaking their hearts. So I am fair itching to hear what young George Dent, twelfth Earl of Leland, has done. Lady Quayle takes an important breath. 'The reason, Tabitha says, for breaking off her engagement to George is that . . . *she does not love him.*' Her poor eyes bulge so hard from staring I fear her head will burst. 'She does not love him! I ask you!' she exclaims, forgetting we are hiding from Lord Quayle. 'Have you ever heard of such a thing? She quite fails to see that it is none of her business to *love* him.'

Lady Quayle is quite right. Love has nothing to do with it. Tabitha must marry well and leave romance out of it – she has a large family fortune to think of, and a good aristocratic name. That's what you get for being a lady.

'She has likely been reading too many novels,' she says ruefully. For a moment she looks as if she will cry, and I feel a little sorry for her. 'I must tell you frankly, Miss Rose, I am at my wit's end. Lord Quayle will not speak to her, or myself, about it. I fear he will wash his hands of the matter entirely and send her away, or perhaps even disinherit her, God forbid it! Tabitha is his last child, you see, and he has never liked her. Indeed, he lost all interest in any of the girls after our son Wilfred was born.' She winds her lace handkerchief around her desperate hands, casts her eyes up to heaven, and then at me, pleading, 'I do not know which way to turn, Miss Rose. What to do for the best? I must have you read Tabitha's fortune. I simply cannot go on another day without knowing what is to become of her.'

*

The roll-call at Lady Quayle's next 'mystic *soirée*' is just as before, with the addition of a new face. New, that is, to the wonders of the Romani fortune-telling arts, and, as far as she knows, to this dark gypsy girl. But, though I am new to her, I know her straight away. For I saw her only last week, dressed in pale pink satin to match her flushed cheeks, gazing out over the dance-floor at the Argyll Rooms, while her young gent made advances under the table to her friend, Miss Emily, who is here tonight also.

'This, my dear Miss Rose, is my daughter Tabitha,' says Lady Quayle, with such a heavy note of significance I fear she will wink at me. 'She was so disappointed to have missed our last gathering that I felt I must bring us together for another. I have told her all about your extraordinary talents.' Again that almost-wink: I swear I can see my lady's eye twitching with the effort to stop herself.

'I am delighted to make your acquaintance, Miss Rose,' says Tabitha. 'Indeed, I was quite maddened to have missed your last visit. Mama has told me how very clever you are.'

'Oh, it's true,' chimes in Greedy Girl. I remember her from last time, though I forget her name. 'Madam Rose is very good. The last time she told me I would receive an invitation, that Thursday, for the Goldsmiths' dinner. And that I must go, for it was there that I should meet my prospective fiancé.' She draws a breath, as if keeping the company on tenterhooks, though they look only faintly interested. I reckon they find themselves listening to a deal of her news and are weary of it. 'Lord Arthur Brocklebank,' she says, at last, with a flourish of her hand. No one seems impressed. She has taken such a time to tell us that I think some have forgotten the last thing she said and have no idea how Lord Arthur Brocklebank might be significant here. 'And, indeed, she was right!' exclaims Greedy Girl, beaming at me. 'Quite right, in every detail.'

Now, I do recall predicting a grand dinner invitation, for I remember thinking that she really didn't need another grand dinner. Though I don't believe I specified the day, or the Goldsmiths, or indeed Lord Arthur Brocklebank.

'My palm is fairly itching to be read again,' she declares,

holding it, coyly folded behind her fat fingers, to her fluttering heart.

'Is that right, my dear?' I say. 'Then perhaps you had better go first. If it's all the same to our gracious hostess, of course.'

'Oh, yes, of course,' says Greedy Girl, looking hungrily at Lady Quayle.

'Please,' says our gracious lady. 'Do as you think fit.'

*

There is nothing new in Greedy Girl's hand, except a little more padding around her fingers. I should tell her it would benefit her to take up tennis, or badminton, at least. Or to eat less cake. But I do not. I tell her she is coming upon a fork in the road, a dividing of the way, that it is time to take stock of her prospects. She doesn't like this as well as dinner invitations.

'But what of Lord Brocklebank?' she says.

I tell her not to count her chickens. When I look along her Vital line into the future, I see her blowing up like a balloon.

After Greedy Girl comes our hostess. She enters the room as if we were playing at not knowing one another – though there is no one else to see us – only she wears a little smile at the corners of her mouth that says she has a connection to me that sets her just above the others, ahead of the game.

This time I pore over Lady Quayle's palm as if it was a work as complex and mysterious as the Holy Bible itself. In fact, it is a fairly simple hand, though criss-crossed by tiny lines of worry.

'Hmm,' I say to myself, and then, 'Ah' – I whip out my optical glass for further effect. After two or three minutes I can feel her busting her stays to ask me what I see.

'You have a very deep hand, my lady,' I tell her, at last. Which means nothing at all, but pleases her thoroughly. 'Every time I look at it I see something new.'

'Oh!' she says, flattered. 'And what do you see this evening?'

'I see a halo around the Saturnian line, at its crossing with the Mensal . . .' she peers at her palm curiously, although she has no idea which lines these are – a good thing, there being no halo to see '. . . so faint that I did not take proper account of it before.'

'Do you?' she asks, her brow furrowing. 'And what does that mean?'

Poor Lady Quayle. Her pale, open face in the candlelight looks sad, perhaps a little lonely. The strain of these last few weeks seems to weigh so very heavy on her. She must feel helpless indeed as she watches her reckless, rebellious daughter throw away the prospect of a good match for such a foolish notion as love – likely she is wondering where she has gone wrong with her and how she can make it right, and feeling she is losing her daughter, somehow. So, perhaps, a sense of gaining a new one, in some way, might be of some small comfort.

'This halo is very rare,' I tell her. 'Taken in conjunction with the star below your Saturn finger, I would say that it marks you out as – well! A Good Samaritan, if you like . . .'

'Indeed?' says Lady Quayle, pleased as Punch. 'A Good Samaritan, you say?'

'Someone who has a great and natural capacity for giving, Lady Quayle.'

'Well,' says she, 'I do have my charitable activities . . .'

'But this, my good lady, is something else altogether.' I take a solemn breath and lean in to her a little, frowning with the effort of serious thought. 'These marks,' I tell her, 'point to you as no less than the personal architect of some poor soul's salvation.'

Lady Quayle looks up from her hand with wide, pious eyes. I have her hook, line and sinker.

'I myself have never seen this combination,' I say, shaking my head in wonder, as if Halley's Comet had just flown past. 'My grandmother told me of it, and she saw it only once in her long life. These marks are found only in the palms of very great philanthropists or, indeed . . . saints.' This last word hangs for a moment in the air before an impressive silence falls around us like a stage curtain.

'Goodness me,' murmurs Lady Quayle, at last, and suddenly I realize that this is the first time for a long while – perhaps ever – that she has been told anything special or remarkable about herself. And though it is a lie, I feel have done her a service. She digests this new vision of her holy ladyship for a short while, gazing before her as if it were hanging in the air there, which, indeed, gives her something of the look of the aforementioned saints. Then a frown clouds her beatific brow. 'But how am I to fulfil this calling?' she says.

'Time will tell, my lady.'

'Oh,' she says, disappointed.

'Time . . . or, perhaps, the crystal ball.'

'The crystal ball?' she echoes, perking up.

'Would my lady like me to have a look into the mystic crystal?'

'Have you brought one?' she says, lighting up like a child before a sweetshop window.

'I have, my lady. But only for you. You must tell no one else about it.'

'Oh, no,' she says. 'No, of course.'

Now then, I have no talent for the crystal ball. But I am not about to tell Lady Quayle that. If it is the crystal ball she wants, and is prepared to pay extra for, I can give it a try. It's the very least I can do. I am respectable enough at the cards, but she doesn't want me to read those – I expect they are not exotic enough for her liking. No, nothing but the mystic crystal will do.

So we begin. I unwrap the crystal ball from its black velvet cloth, lay it out on the table before the candle flame, and incant a Romani spell as her eyes grow wider and wider.

Ekkeri, akai-ri, u kair-an.
Fillissin, follasi, Nakelas ja'n

I stare into the depths of the crystal. We hold our breath. Nothing appears, much like the last time I tried it. I can hear my grandmother's voice in my ear – *Don't stare so girl*, she says. *Let it come.* I close my eyes and there is a smell of beeswax, and tobacco, and laundry soap, and the jangle of silver coins in her pocket, cut glass tinkling on shelves. I open my eyes again. *Don't stare so. Let it come.*

'Can you see a poor wretched soul?' asks Lady Quayle. The painted wagon vanishes around me and there is just the scent of rosewater, and beef brisket boiling downstairs. My good lady is fairly twitching in her seat, bursting with questions, so keen is she to begin her career as saviour of this lost soul whose deliverance is her destiny. I fix her with a mysterious gaze. 'Have patience,' I tell her. 'The crystal must reveal these secrets in its own good time.'

Lady Quayle is a kind enough woman but she must have guidance, having not much in the way of a mind to call her own, and so there is no danger of her going out under her own steam to find poor souls to save, such as sit on every corner. No, our good lady will not shirk the task Fate has set aside for her, and readies herself to give generously as soon as the recipient is named. Only who is she? What part of London Town might she frequent? In what wretched hovel might she be found?

'The Haymarket, my lady.'

'The Haymarket?'

'I see the Haymarket, clear as day.'

'And what else?' She waits, holding her breath.

'No, my lady, it's gone. The Haymarket is all Fate will tell us for now.'

'Do you not see a number?'

'All in good time, my lady. All will be revealed, in good time. The mystic crystal does not give up its revelations all at once. We must only be patient until our next meeting'.

Though we may be burning with frustrated charity!

The rest of the party follow, much as before, not much new to tell among them. Each time the door opens I am hoping it will be the new member of the mystic gaggle.

34

And at last she comes, with her piece of silver, a crown no less. She must be hoping for good news. As she crosses my palm with it, I take in her smooth knuckles, the pale, aristocratic skin on the back of her hand, the sheen of pearls around her wrist. Three strings of them, fastened with a clasp in the shape of a heart.

Well, I can see straight off why Miss Tabitha Quayle might be found supping cold sham on the balcony at the Argyll Rooms. She has a smooth, fleshy palm, clear lines, fingers that bend outward at the last phalange, revealing a carefree, adventurous bent to her character, a plump Venus mount, denoting passion, a wavering Cerebral line to show that she really takes nothing seriously at all. Her short little finger says you won't see her in a library. And she has the reckless pointed Saturn finger of those with an impetuous heart and a stormy temper. But I don't tell her this in so many words.

I tell her she has a taste for the exotic that may get her into trouble. That though she doesn't much care for books it may profit her to read. That she must not take too much pepper. And that this branch from the Mount of the Moon means an unexpected journey is in store for her. Her ears prick up at that. 'An unexpected journey?' she says. 'Will it be soon?'

'Yes,' I tell her, 'quite soon.'

Her eyes widen a little, and she opens her mouth as if to ask something, but evidently thinks better of it, and closes it again.

There are two things I do not mention at all. The first is a little dark spot on the Mensal line, or line of the heart, that marks those whose sorry hearts belong to philanderers. Well, I'll wager I know who he is. And the other thing . . .

Well, I have to look at the other mark twice to see it is really true, and then again through the optical glass. A tiny star on the Mount of Mars. Accompanied by a narrow quadrangle and a broad, straight Mensal line.

It marks a killer. This girl, with her golden curls and her rosy cheeks.

Murder, it says. *Horrid, bloody murder.*

I set her hand back down upon the lace cloth – a little too quickly, I think, for she looks at me and, for a moment, I think she is going to ask me what I have seen. Perhaps she knows already. We look at each other across the tabletop. If Tabitha Quayle knows her own dark secret she hides it well. She smiles, pretty as a picture – if I hadn't seen into her heart I might never have noticed the little steely flash in her blue eyes: cold and hard, like wet stones. Indeed, I might have thought that I imagined it.

'Thank you, Miss Rose,' she says, and gets up. I watch her cross the room, with delicate steps, on dainty feet.

I feel rather pale, though a quick look in the glass shows me bold enough. If only that was all of them done. But it is not. There is the last to come, and who else could it be but Emily? I don't see her enter, but she is there, suddenly, stood inside the door, behind me. I see her reflection in the mirror, start a little and spin round.

'I do beg your pardon, miss,' she says.

We sit down, and Emily crosses my palm with a shilling. This time she extends her hand across the cloth without hesitation.

As I take up that pale, soft little paw I am hoping that cross, the cross on the Saturnian line, will be gone – it was only a tiny thing after all, faint, and barely there. Perhaps it will have disappeared, or any one of its attendant omens.

But there it is, clear as day. Clearer, even, than before. And there too is the grille on the Mount of Mars, the sloping line, the second little cross on the Rascette. And now, instead of those thousand fearful, violent deaths beginning to play in my imagination, there is only one. Or, rather, the fearful death has only one face, and it is a flushed, laughing one, with golden hair and cold blue eyes, like wet stones. I look up into Emily's neat, serious face, framed with that tight mouse-brown hair and I wonder how to put it to her.

'You must be very careful,' I tell her. And it seems a very poor thing to say.

'Careful?' she says. 'Of what?'

I have opened my mouth to tell her, 'Everything', when I realize how absurd it will sound and so I close it again. I have never been caught short for words before. The things I might say whirl in my head like dead leaves, but still I sit and look at that square little hand, slightly rough, with its closed fingers. She is not a lady, our Emily, not like her fashionable friends. She comes from a modest home and works for her living: not as hard as a maid perhaps, but she works all right. I expect I should find her in a draper's shop or a druggist's on Oxford Street. And I wonder if her fancy friends talk about it among themselves, about her modest means and her job and her plain grey dress and her tight mousy hair. Perhaps they are talking about it even now, behind their hands in the other room, while she is in here with me.

When I look up again at Emily Mouse's face, it is quite composed. She seems a hundred years old and I think to myself that I have no call to feel sorry for her, that she can brush the barbed attentions of her catty friends aside with a wave of her little grey tail. I pull her hand nearer to the candle and take up my optical glass. I must find something useful to tell her.

And there, as I scan the hills and valleys of Miss Emily's hand, is a tiny crescent: high on the Mount of the Moon, perfect, and clear of all the other lines, as if it had landed there. Beware, it says. *Beware the fatal influence of a woman.*

'Beware?' says Emily. I leave out the 'fatal' part.

'Beware the influence of a woman.' She looks at me sharply then. Quite a different shade draws over Emily's face. And I'll wager she knows which woman that would be.

A fair-haired creature with flushed rosy cheeks and ice-blue eyes.

'A woman?' she says.

'Yes.'

Chapter Three

Rose

'I have been to the Haymarket,' announces Lady Quayle, at our next meeting, as I set out the crystal ball. 'What a dreadful place it is.'

'Yes indeed, my lady.'

'I really cannot believe I have been so close to it all these years and never taken note of it. But, then, I suppose I have never, before last week, seen it after dark.'

'Indeed, it becomes quite a different prospect once the gas is lit.'

'Do you know it, my dear?'

'I know it is a quagmire of dubious morality, my lady, swarming with unlikely women and rogues of the lowest order: card sharps, blacklegs and thieves. The worst of them come out after midnight – so I have heard – to ply their evil business and drink into the early hours of the morning. Any decent person would be a fool to set foot there after that hour.'

'After midnight?' she exclaims. 'Good gracious me. Do they never go to bed?'

'They sleep in the hours of daylight, so I believe, my lady.'

'It is a veritable sea of lost souls,' she remarks to herself, with some satisfaction. 'A heaving ocean of iniquity. Do you know, upon my visit I had intended to alight from the carriage and explore the area on foot, but once I saw how the crowd swelled and shoved, spilling over the flagstones into the road, and heard how they shouted and swore – such talk as I have never heard in my life! – I decided to remain inside it.'

'Very wise, my lady.'

'Yes indeed,' she says. Then she purses her lips and looks at me sideways. 'I do wonder, Miss Rose,' she says, after a short pause for thought, 'how I am to find this poor lost girl in such a rabble – and, indeed, what it will be, so very particularly, that will mark her out as the girl I am looking for. It seems to me that there are very many souls in the Haymarket that are wanting salvation.'

'An ocean of them, my lady.'

'Yes,' she says doubtfully. She looks as though she is wondering suddenly if it is such a fine idea after all.

'Hmm,' I murmur, waving my hands over the crystal ball, making the candle upon the black cloth flicker and shine on its surface. 'Perhaps, Lady Quayle, the particular thing about this soul, the one poor, lost girl whose destiny is linked in the stars with your own is that . . . But wait . . . I see her now: on the steps of an imposing building, perchance a theatre . . . yes, a theatre, I see a fancy silk dress . . . Ah! She is gone.' Lady Quayle is hanging on my every word. As I look up from the crystal she draws breath again. 'Perhaps, my lady, the thing about this girl is that she is the one – and indeed the only – redeemable soul among that devilish throng.'

Wide-eyed, she digests these words, evidently not having entertained the idea before that the Haymarket crowd may not be lining up to be saved; at least, not on Lady Quayle's terms, which shall certainly involve parades of attendance at church for the benefit of their lady saviour's acquaintances, and testimonials to the enhancement of her reputation.

'Yes,' she says, 'I see.'

'And as to how you will find each other,' I tell her, 'I am certain that Fate, having chosen you to save this poor creature, will put her somewhere you will be able to see her.'

'Do you think so?'

'I am quite sure of it.'

'Well, that is some comfort, after all. Fate does work in mysterious ways,' she says, with a little satisfied sigh.

'Fate, my lady – and God.'

'God! Yes, of course.' She'd forgotten about Him. Now she looks sheepish.

'It seems we are due some more clues, my lady,' I venture. 'Shall we look again?'

I see a girl, not a young creature but not yet too far gone over, a dear creature with a faithful, lost heart, hidden behind a garish façade of fancy silk . . . I see black and white . . . stripes! Yes indeed, clear as day, I see her! In a striped dress, with a red rosette at her throat. A poor lost heart, behind a smiling face, sitting on the steps of the Theatre Royal . . .

'Can you tell what day it is?' asks my dear lady.

Is it possible that she has asked me such a thing? And what in Creation am I to answer to a question such as this?

'It is hard to say, Lady Quayle. I shall guess at Thursday. Thursday may be the day.' This seems to satisfy her well enough. She sighs contentedly as I wrap the crystal ball back into its cloth. We are quiet then for some moments, as the question that has been plaguing me all week turns in my mind. Eventually I spit it out, as nonchalantly as I can.

'What of the girls, my lady, if I may enquire after them?'

'The girls?'

'Your dear daughter, how is she?' I ask her. 'And her friend – is it Emily? What news of them?'

'Tabitha is well enough, Miss Rose. It is kind of you to ask. And Emily . . .'

'Yes?'

'Well, Emily is just as she always is!' She smiles benevolently. 'Busying around her dear little shop, poor thing. I saw her only this morning.'

Only this morning. The words quiet the thought that swirls around my head every time I lay it on my pillow. That night I sleep without dreaming. Life is like streaky bacon. There is fat, and there is lean. If you tell fortunes you must take them together. And fortunes may change their course – or what matter choice, what purpose in rising, and dressing, moving from here to there?

*

'Now, then, Lillie, my dear,' I ask, 'are you ready to be saved on Thursday?'

Miss Lillie Daley mulls this over for as long as it takes her to scrape another oyster's foot from its shell and tip it down her throat. 'Well, I've a lot on this week, Rose,' she says, licking her fingers. 'I've three important guests to see to and a very busy party. Couldn't my salvation begin next week instead?'

'She's very eager, my dear. If she can't start by Thursday or so, I fear she may up and find herself another wretched soul. Or give over the idea altogether.'

'Very well,' she says. 'I shall have to fit it in.'

'Good girl. It'll be worth your while.'

'I haven't been saved since April last. I hope I shall remember the routine.'

'Now you're talking nonsense.'

'And mayn't I be perhaps getting a little bit old for this caper? She might think I'm beyond saving.'

'Of course not. Twenty-four you may be but you've still enough of a bloom on your evil cheek. Indeed, we shall have to powder you down to make you wan and wretched enough.'

*

I see nothing of Emily, or Tabitha, for the next few days, not at the Argyll Rooms or anywhere else, but I find them in my thoughts again – one, then the other, and then together they start to swirl with their mysterious philanderer, holding both their hands under the table. And though I try to put them aside, they twist and spin in my head as I wonder what will become of them, and if it is becoming at that very moment.

The next thing I hear about any of them is from Lady Quayle, late on Thursday evening, when she summons me to be consulted on pressing business. It is getting dark as Mrs Bunion calls up to announce the footman. This time I accompany him straight back to Cavendish Square.

Lady Quayle is brimming with news. She has found the girl! On the steps of the Theatre Royal, would you believe? Dressed in striped silk, with a red rosette at her throat. Well! Lady Quayle had fairly dropped down dead when she saw her there – indeed, she was so overcome she found herself unable to approach, or speak to the girl but, rather, resolved on the spot never to make a move without consulting me first. I am overwhelmed at this vote of confidence. But not taken aback in the least at the appearance of the girl, on the steps, with her red rosette. After all, I saw it, clear as crystal, in the mysterious gypsy ball. And Lady Quayle, if she thought about it, would be disappointed if I seemed surprised, or even so much as pleased at this unfolding of my own predictions. It would be as if I was making it all up as I went along! So it is easy to dispatch this topic of conversation with a straight face.

I oblige her with a reading – just a short one. Just long enough to see the new line that branches out from the Saturnian: a tiny, faint line, that marks the beginning of a most favourable new endeavour. Indeed, I can see my lady's good reputation growing before my very eyes. Of course, she doesn't care about that at all, really, but only for the well-being and moral salvation of the girl with the red rosette – poor lost creature that she is, strayed so far from the path.

When she asks me how best to proceed with her good works I tell her one can only hope to save a soul after securing salvation of the body. When she looks bewildered, I say that this lamb needs a living, off the street, before it can be returned to the flock. When my lady looks a little vague still (she isn't the sharpest knife in the drawer), I tell her that the girl needs her lodgings paid for, and her food, and money for new clothes – I would guess at a hundred pounds. After all, she can't very well be saved with a red rosette around her neck, can she now? With a last glance across Lady Quayle's palm I note the strengthening of her halo.

And then I ask her, quite casually again, what news of her lovely daughter Tabitha.

'Tabitha is quite well, thank you,' she says. She looks vacant for a moment, as if she had forgotten all about her, and the troubles that were so pressing only a few days ago. I am getting round to asking after Miss Emily when she decides to tell me more. 'As a matter of fact, Miss Rose, I have decided not to fret a moment longer on her account – or, rather, on account of the ridiculous Dent business. To be truthful, I never cared much for the match. She is only seventeen, after all, and has plenty of time to find another suitor. Indeed, she has the very good fortune to have attracted the attentions of the Herberts' son, just this Monday gone, at the spring ball, and we have high hopes for this new connection. He is coming to call on her a week on Friday.'

'Well my lady, what very good news that is,' I say politely, though I am thinking that – well, they didn't waste any time and that you might call it indecent, and how little there is to choose between the Quayle ladies and the Haymarket ladies when you boil down to the bones of it.

'Yes! Isn't it?' She beams. 'They are a very good family, the Herberts. Much better than the Dents, in fact. Do you know their father is both the Earl of Pembroke *and* of Montgomery?

I have great expectations of them.' She tilts her airy head and gazes out over the garden. I imagine her fanciful thoughts like little French cakes, sliding off their stand, across the empty space and out of the window. Suddenly an idea seems to seize her.

It's a wonder she hasn't asked before.

'You've read Tabitha's hand, Miss Rose. What does it say?'

'What it says today I do not know, my lady. And I couldn't tell you if I did.'

'Oh.' She doesn't press me on the matter. Perhaps, deep down, she doesn't want to know.

'Well, anyhow,' she says, 'I shall be free of my responsibilities towards her for two whole weeks come tomorrow morning, and mean to devote myself to this creature with the red rosette.'

'Oh, Lady Quayle? Two weeks?'

'Yes indeed! She is leaving for St Leonards, near Hastings, tomorrow, to enjoy some rest and fresh air before the season begins in earnest. She is taking a friend to accompany her – you remember Emily, from our *soirées*? Such a funny little thing, we all feel rather sorry for her. She's from quite good stock, not that you'd think it to look at her, only her father was a gambler and lost the family fortune, every last bean of it, modest as it was. At that he had the decency to hang himself – the very least he could do, one could be forgiven for thinking. Anyhow, his poor family set to managing as best they could under their sorry circumstances. It was Tabitha who found her first, just off Oxford Street, in a draper's shop! Can you imagine the indignity of it? And so we do make every effort to be kind to her, in any way we can be – hence Tabitha's selfless gesture, in choosing her as travelling companion. Emily resisted a little, of course, she is so very proud, but my dear daughter is so very persuasive! She promised to make a little detour to visit Emily's mother – by Beckenham, I believe, or some such place, she has not seen her for a year, you know – and that was what made up Emily's mind to go at last.'

I see Emily's little hand before me on the cloth, every line and mark, like print.

Beware the fatal influence of a woman.

'Dear Tabitha. Such a kind thing to do. Even a shopgirl deserves a holiday!' With these portentous words ringing in my ears, I prepare to take my leave of Lady Quayle.

We have a little scheme by which I come and go without attracting the attentions of the staff – it seems Lord Quayle has instructed them to keep an eye on his wife's activities and report back to him any mysterious callers, queer meetings, crystal balls, rabbit's feet, Ouija boards or, indeed, any dark gypsy types within five miles of Cavendish Square. And who can blame him?

So, she calls for coffee, and then again, for clean linen for the large guest room, and then she sends my friend the footman out to Fortnum & Mason, to pick her up some candied ginger, while I hide behind the curtain. Once the butler is busy in the kitchen, and the maid upstairs, and the footman grumbling his way down Regent Street, I am to slip out by the scullery door. And so the plan goes off.

Until, that is, I reach the lower stairs and go to tiptoe past the kitchen. For someone else is at the scullery door. Someone in a silk dress, with golden hair in ringlets. The door is open and Miss Tabitha Quayle is whispering to somebody on the other side of it, urgently, casting furtive looks back at the kitchen. I stop, still. The cook and butler are deep in conversation about the dinner menu. The butler wants to serve boiled fowls *à la Béchamel* with the loin of veal for the second course. Cook says there are only two, and it won't be sufficient for ten. Is Cook not doing the knuckle of ham as well? the butler wants to know. Well, of course she is, what does he take her for?

I go to slip into the pantry till Miss Tabitha is gone. But I am too slow. She turns, sees me and starts – her hand goes behind her back with the secret letter it is holding. And there we stand and stare each other down. I can see the wheels turning in her fair head as she wonders how long I have been there behind her, what I have heard. I hear the clock ticking behind those hard blue eyes. Killer's eyes, like cold wet stones.

The butler wonders who's in charge of the ordering, and Cook tells him he knows very well, but it isn't her fault if the butcher sends the wrong things and she'd thank him not to mention it again. I press a finger to my lips, and at that Miss Tabitha Quayle steps away from the door, brushes past me and glides up the stairs without a sound.

*

Out in the street I lean on a railing, let my thrashing heart recover itself. All my fears for Miss Emily Mouse seem to rise up again and swallow me.

I must send word to Lady Quayle. Miss Tabitha must not take Emily away with her: the excursion must be stopped.

I write a letter as soon as I can lay my hands upon paper and pen:

My dear Lady Quayle
I must warn you urgently that Miss Tabitha's trip to the country is a most ill-starred venture. If you cannot persuade her to abandon it, at least she must not go with Emily. I urge you in the strongest terms to prevent it.

But then I picture Lady Quayle, flapping her hands and fussing, following Miss Tabitha around her room, as she prepares her bags, with deranged tales of doom, unlucky stars and dire warnings, and I think how unable she is to prevent her daughter doing anything. And how the girl will know that it comes from me, and imagine there is something fishy in it. And so I continue:

It is best you speak to Emily herself. She must be warned directly

Warned? Of what? Of course I can't tell Lady Quayle the truth of it. That under her fair ringlets and her pale pink satin gown her daughter is a murderess. No!

*if she is to avoid the dreadful fate I have seen unfolding in
the crystal ball. I can say nothing more about it here, but
only trust that you will see it done. And may God bless
you for it.*

Rose

I read it over. It seems clear enough. But now I wonder
how much Lady Quayle will care about what becomes of
Emily, and if she does care – enough to warn her off – how
easy it will be for a shopgirl to give up a holiday.

*

I receive a reply late that very afternoon.

My dear Rose,

*All is done as you directed. I have been straight to Miss
Emily's shop and told her myself. At first I must admit she
seemed somewhat offended, until I explained to her that it
was in no way to do with the disparity between Tabitha's
social position and her own, but instead a matter of ill-
omen, written in the stars, and who could argue with
that? Fret not, my dear.*

Yours, Margaret, Lady Quayle

I find this message very much less reassuring than it was
intended to be. In fact, I am afraid that Lady Quayle may
have done nothing more than embarrass our poor shopgirl.
I think, for a rash moment, I may look for Emily near Oxford
Street until I remember how very long it is, and how many

shops there are, and how strangely Emily will think it if I turn up at her work to warn her off her trip – I, a fortune-teller, whom she barely knows! – and realize what a ridiculous notion it is. I must pull myself together. I have done all I can for Emily. But I feel strange, as I sit downstairs in the Buttered Bun, pushing boiled potatoes around my plate.

I feel as if someone is walking over my grave, and I do not like it.

*

The next morning is fair and bright: summer is lighting up London Town. Crocuses are pushing up their heads in the beds of Soho Square, the milkman whistles a cheery tune. Mrs Bunion fetches me up a cup of coffee.

'Has anyone been with a letter?' I ask her.

'No, dear,' she says. 'No one this morning.' She looks down over the square, this way and that. 'We haven't seen that footman for a few days now,' she says, almost ruefully, as if she missed his surly face. 'He'll have me worrying about him if he doesn't come soon. Perhaps he's been crushed under the wheels of a cart! Or fallen down a hole.'

'His mistress has taken him off post duties, Mrs B. He's too thick with the butler. And everything gets back from him in turn to the master of the house.'

'Oh,' she says. 'No. I expect the master doesn't like you there.'

'You're about right, Mrs B. Though he's never clapped eyes on me, thank goodness. He's out at his club every day. I should be afraid of him.'

'I expect he thinks it's all a lot of nonsense, does he?'

'And who can blame him?'

'Mm.' We watch a small dog shitting in the very centre of the square. 'It must be a funny thing though,' she says, 'for our poor lady, skulking and creeping about in her own house. Imagine that! Skulking and creeping around in fear of your old man. I couldn't bear it. Do you know, Rose, I'm happier in a little house like this than a great big mansion any day of the week – nice and cosy, with Mr Bunion upstairs in his room. And I can come and go as I please, you see, and if he didn't like it, well, I'd give him a good kick, and that'd be an end of it.' She nods firmly, just the once, to put a full stop to this solid sentiment and swallows the last of her coffee. 'Well, dear, if you'll excuse me I must get back to my buns.'

I watch the small dog lift its leg on a lamp post before rounding the corner, and stare into the square at nothing in particular. And there it is again, that thought: is Tabitha gone to St Leonard's yet? Is Emily with her? There they are, bobbing up in front of my face, driving me mad. I must wash and dress, and go about the day's business. I must trust that Lady Quayle has dealt with it.

And then, just as if I had summoned it, a carriage rolls into Soho Square from Oxford Street. I have seen it before. There on the seat is my friend the surly footman. Has he come for me? I almost call out to Mrs Bunion that he is here, right as rain, not fallen down a hole after all, but the carriage sweeps by, with no sign of slowing. I catch a glimpse inside the cab as it rushes past. There sit two women: a fair, ringleted creature and, beside her, a little grey mouse. The clatter of the wheels on the cobbled road sounds like rifle shots, avalanches of rocks. The blood surges to my ears and my heart bangs a drum in my chest as I leap to my feet and cry after them, 'WAIT! MISS EMILY! WAIT!'

But they are gone. I stare as the carriage rounds the corner and disappears, my breath ragged, knuckles white around the window frame.

*

Lady Quayle tells me she did her utmost to stop them: she spoke to Emily, herself, at the shop, and told her everything I had said, and Emily assured her that she wouldn't go.

'Perhaps she wanted to be left alone at work and only said what my lady wanted to hear,' I suggest, wondering at how a lady can let a gypsy girl speak to her in this manner.

'Oh. Do you really suppose so?' she says, crestfallen. 'But why in heaven would she do that?'

'Perhaps she was overwhelmed by your concern, my lady. I do not expect Emily likes to draw attention to herself. She is only a shopgirl after all.'

'No, indeed.'

'And perhaps it is altogether too hard for a shopgirl to forfeit a holiday.'

'Yes, I see.' She knits her powdered brow. Thinking is not something I have seen Lady Quayle do before at any length, and this time is no different – the next moment she has brightened up again. 'Ah, well!' she says. 'She does work very hard, poor dear. I expect she deserves one.' She beams, as if the holiday were all her doing. 'Now,' she says, 'I intend to seek out the Haymarket girl this very afternoon. At what hour do you think I might find her?'

I have no need to look into the crystal ball to tell her that.

'I would say six o'clock is likely, my lady. Before the crowd becomes too thick.'

'Indeed. They are a fearful rabble. And how much did you say would be enough to set the girl up to begin with?'

*

'I wouldn't spare it another thought,' says Lillie, as she calls for more champagne. 'What's this girl to you anyhow – what's her name? Emily. Well, everybody has to go some day, don't they?'

'Lillie!' I scold her. 'How can you say such a thing?'

'Oh, Rose, for heaven's sake,' she says. 'What's bitten you? You're spoiling our supper.' She pulls the leg off a roast pheasant. 'Whatever is the point of coming to Verrey's if you're going to carp on about these silly girls? We'd do just as well to get a boiled sheep's head and go straight home.'

True enough. And what am I to do about any of it, anyhow? All of a sudden I remember something that my grandmother told me, long ago, when I was just a tiny thing. I can see her, by the fire, looking up at the stars. 'It's a curse, sometimes,' she said. 'A gift, and a curse, to see the future. To read disaster, ill-omens, death in people's hands. It's not for you to stand in the way of it.'

'Streaky bacon,' I say, out loud, though I was only thinking it to myself.

'Eh?' says Lillie, with her mouth full.

'Never mind.'

Lillie stops mid-chew to look me in the eye, to be sure I am shaking off this dreary cast – she looks as if she might dish me up a slap if I don't. I smile at her and drain my glass. 'Now,' she says. 'What about our good lady? She's a bubble head, all right! It's a good thing I've a hard heart.'

'Our good lady has never been so happily occupied, my dear. She has a husband who lives at his club and a daughter who no sooner comes home than she goes again. They leave her all alone in that great quiet house, with only the servants to see to and a few dull friends for company, no business of her own to go about – you might say, indeed, no purpose at all – when there you are, poor wretched girl, waiting for her to busy herself with you. She fair lit up this morning at the prospect of taking you off these evil streets. You may count yourself as doing her a goodly service.'

'Well, there's a thing to gladden the heart. Here's to it, Miss Rose.'

'Here's to you, Miss Annie Atkins! You poor fallen wretch, you!'

We clink our glasses together, drops of sham jumping from them, catching the light from the chandelier. 'How far up the garden path do you reckon to go?'

'We shall see, my dear. One step at a time. I hope you've kept that brown worsted dress in mothballs.'

'It's not a day older. Ugly thing. The moths wouldn't eat it if you served it *à la Maître d'Hotel*, with custard.'

'Very good.'

'It's not you has to wear it.'

*

On Monday brave Miss Lillie puts on Annie Atkins' dull brown dress and meets her benefactress in Regent Circus. She thanks her for her kind attentions, shows her the modest worsted daygown she has bought with her ladyship's money and tells her she has taken rooms in Dean Street, which, though nice enough for a common girl like her, are much too humble to receive her ladyship. But oh! The blessed relief of having her own quarters, where she may lie upon her own bed without fear of a visit from her wicked taskmaster: a devil, who – though she spares her good mistress the details of their association – Lady Quayle can imagine only too well, with his growling visage, his rough murderous hands. She shudders to think of the fate from which she has delivered this unfortunate and gives herself a little pat on the back for her pains. And now, if only Miss Annie Atkins can keep herself off the streets – for they are a way of life to which she is accustomed, and as soon as hardship shows his face at the door again, knowing no other way, she will be struggling not to tread them again – if only she can keep herself upon the righteous path, she vows to spread the word to other fallen girls, and turn them from the road to Hell.

*

Lady Quayle was not lying when she swore she would never make another move without my advice. The poor footman arrives before breakfast three times that week, to ask, variously, would lilac be an inauspicious colour to wear for horse riding? Would *Filet de Boeuf à la Jardinière* be an auspicious thing to serve to ten on Wednesday, or would it be better on Saturday evening, to eight? – and, having had the chrysanthemums (especially unlucky, being so very yellow, as they were) removed from the gardens, would it be prudent to take up those in the square, or may they be safely left? I answer these queries no, Saturday, and yes, take up any chrysanthemums you see or, indeed, any yellow plants at all.

Lady Quayle is giving up her own free will, piece by piece, at every fork in the road, surrendering to the whim of Fate. A cynical person could say she might as well defer to the tossing of a coin.

And that week, as I look into the crystal ball, I see a hundred things awaiting Lady Quayle upon the cobbled road of Fate. I see a red rosette, cast aside, lying in the gutter. I see the girl, dressed in modest brown flannel, a Bible in her hand. She walks the busy Haymarket, stops to lend some poor soul a hand out of the gutter. Now I see her upon a box, in Leicester Square, preaching the Gospel – the crowd swirls by her, someone stops to jeer and throw a stone – but here, a fallen girl listens at her feet, just one, and then another, and when she falls down from exhaustion they pick her up and lead her to her lodgings. I see her then, taking them in, poor homeless creatures, sharing her supper, such as it is, soup and dry bread, and at the day's end I see her thanking the Lord her God for her benefactress, her good lady, who delivered her from sin and keeps her so that she may do His work. And then I see the good lady herself: she is at dinner – it is not altogether clear. I see a well-appointed dining room, large, fine indeed, such as the gentry keep, or royalty . . . and there, there is . . . Could it be our prime minister? He is addressing the illustrious company, he nods towards my lady . . . Now he raises his glass, they follow him in the toast . . .

'Goodness!' says Lady Quayle, once I have finished. 'But is the poor girl only eating soup? She must have something better than that, most especially if she is to have guests.'

*

'Here,' says Lillie, palming me a bunch of folded notes across the tablecloth. 'She's a kind woman, our good lady, so she is. Though she asks a lot of questions.'

'What do you think to roping in a couple of local girls, my dear?' I ask her. 'To hear the Word of the Lord, you know, testify to your goodly works, and how you've turned them from the devil's way to Salvation. They'd only have to sit at your feet for half an hour, look repentant when our lady comes by. You could do it somewhere quiet. Say the graveyard? At the back of St Martin's?'

'Pearl's the girl,' says Miss Lillie. 'And May Shearer. They'll do it for a crown.'

*

And then, on Thursday, I have the unexpected pleasure of a call from my friend the surly footman. I am taking coffee downstairs when he appears like a bright blue raincloud at the counter. He looks, in his own surly way, rather pleased with himself, as if he knows something I don't. My heart tightens a little in my chest.

'Good day!' I greet him, as bright as I can muster. He starts and scowls still harder, but also smirks a little at the same time, which surely only he can do. He pulls a letter from his waist-coat and drops it on the tabletop.

'Most urgent, says her ladyship,' he retorts, clipping his words off, short and sparse as he can make them. Indeed, it is the first time he has spoken more than two words to me. And now he has started, the floodgates are open. Though it pains him, he can't resist coughing up a few more.

'There's been proper Bedlam at the house,' he says, with that thin smile as if he was sucking lemon. 'I wonder you've not heard the carry-on all the way down Oxford Street.' He beams down at me suddenly, joyously – all but baring his teeth! It throws me quite off-guard. Clearly he is itching for me to read the letter. For a moment I wonder if Lady Quayle has spotted me dining out with Miss Lillie, but then I know she has not, and I find myself wishing – oh, if only that was it, for I know what is coming.

And I see that the footman is only thinking, Well! You never saw that in your crystal ball, did you?

But of course he is quite wrong, for I have seen it all.

Beware the fatal influence of a woman.

With a thumping heart I open the letter, trying not to tear it.

Rose
  Say you will come at once. I am beside myself with the most wretched news ever a mother could bear. I beg of you to attend me.
  Yours, Margaret, Lady Quayle

The footman watches my shaking hand as I put down the letter. Let him gloat. I ask Mrs Bunion for a nip of brandy.

'Give me five minutes,' I tell him. 'I'll come directly.'

*

In the carriage all the way down Oxford Street my mind is a-whirl. Small wonder Lady Quayle is beside herself. And poor Emily, poor dead Emily! I knew it and did nothing, and though it is not my business to stand in Fate's path yet my bones feel like lead. And what horror did poor Emily suffer? Oh, merciful Heaven let it have been quick and painless! I find I am wringing my hands together. I watch myself as if I was the smirking footman peering through the blind, I see my desolate palms hide my face. What horror! As we roll into Cavendish Square I compose myself as well as I can to face my lady. The carriage stops at the front door, as though she cares nothing any more for who might see me calling. My heart sounds doom in my chest as the butler lets me in.

And there is Lady Quayle, coming towards me: she has heard the door and come out to the hall herself. She reaches me and takes my hands, clings to them, her face a picture of despair.

'Thank the good Lord you could come,' she whispers, her voice breaking. 'Thank you, Rose, thank you.' Her eyes are red-rimmed from weeping, I feel the heaviness of her poor breaking heart, desperate as she grips my fingers, twisting them inside the gloves.

'It is nothing at all, my lady.' I feel I will cry as well.

'Oh, Rose!' she says. 'I hardly need tell you what has befallen us for I know you have seen it and kept it from me out of kindness and a hope it would not come to pass. And then so valiantly tried to prevent it . . . Indeed, I cannot bear to say the words, I fear my heart will break again. If only I had been more vigilant, done my part, we might have escaped these misfortunes . . .'

My lady's voice rises to a wail, filling the great space above our heads, echoing off the cold walls: it is a terrible thing to hear. I feel the household stop around us, the cook hold her breath in the pantry, the maid at the top of the stairs freeze, duster in hand. And I see Emily, in my mind's eye, as if I were looking into the crystal ball – laid out cold and pale, as if made of wax.

'Come, Lady Quayle,' I say. 'Let us talk in private.'

'Yes,' says she, pulling herself together a little. 'Forgive me, Rose. Let us retire upstairs.' She takes my arm and, leaning on it a little, guides me towards the stairs. And then she says something that fairly stops my heart.

'Poor dear Emily is waiting for us there.'

Emily is waiting for us there?

It is no exaggeration to say that, for a moment, I forget completely where I am. My head seems to have left my body: it seems that I am looking down from the ceiling, a hundred feet above these miniature people, all standing oddly in this strange hall for some reason I have lost. And then, for a dreadful moment, I think of poor dear Emily waiting for us laid out on a cold bed, and I wonder why Lady Quayle has had her brought here, and think how very guilty she must feel to torment herself so. All this goes by in the blink of an eye.

And it seems I do well in hiding the whirlwind inside my head, for Lady Quayle says: 'Poor Emily, she saw it all, Rose. I have not told her you are coming, she is too distraught to take it in. She only cries, and looks fitfully out at the window. But I know it will do her good to see you – it will calm her, steady her nerves. Come.' And with little sobs, every fifth step or so, Lady Quayle leads me up the stairs.

Chapter Four

Tabitha

The first time I lay eyes on Valentin I knew that he was to be my destiny. It sounds foolish, I expect, but then I expect I am a foolish girl, and I would not be otherwise. For if I had been sensible to those around me, my responsibilities and, not least, my friend Emily – who was so very dear to me – I would have closed my eyes to his charms, turned my back and never known the joy of true love. And I do believe in true love – one true love, the meeting of two halves that makes the whole. I believe that a life can never be complete without it and that, unjust as it seems, it is the fate of some to wander the earth all their days never to find their intended. And once they are old and ugly, it is their lot to live out the rest of their lives – getting on as best they can – without it. Thus it follows that once one has found one's heart's destiny, it is the most important thing, above all else, to follow him wherever and however one must. And so, you see, what I did to my poor mama was regrettable, but quite unavoidable.

And as for Emily . . . well. It was written in the stars.

Have you ever been inside a painted gypsy wagon? They are the quaintest thing. I used to see them in Kent, as a child, when we left London for the country. If you could have told me then that one day I would take to the road in one, sleep in a bunk bed, sit on the pretty painted steps, by the fire, under the stars, why, I would have woken every morning hoping it would be the day the gypsies came for me. I used to dream about them, with their dark eyes, rings on their fingers, gold in their teeth. It is said that the Roma fall ill if they live in houses; that they must be free to go where the road takes them. Well, that was how I felt in Cavendish Square – that I was shrinking somehow: wasting away, like a bird in a cage.

I dreamed of Valentin, last night. I dreamed he was beside me and it was a dreadful shock to wake and find myself within these four walls again. I know he loves me, wherever he is. I know he looks into the dark sky and prays to God for my deliverance.

It was Emily who brought him to me. He was in the shop one morning, of all the places to find a man! It was very early, there was no one but us to see him – I would always visit at a good hour, usually on a Tuesday morning, before it became too busy, so that we might have a chance to talk while I looked at whatever new things were in that week. Oxford Street was making ready for the crowds but they were still at home in Balham, or Vauxhall, or wherever it is they come from. And in I came, with my head full of nothing at all and my hat a little damp from the spring rain, and there he was, leaning on the counter, with his strong, languid brown hands, and his rough boots. He had a matchstick in his mouth, and a lock of dark hair falling over his forehead, a printed handkerchief knotted around his neck. He looked up as I came in – his eyes were the colour of dark golden honey: they seemed to look right into me, to pierce my very soul – and I stood, frozen on the doormat, struck quite dumb. It was love, at first sight, like Catherine and Heathcliff. Nothing moved, save the lazy matchstick rolling between his shining teeth.

It was Emily who brought me out of my trance. 'Why, Tabitha!' she said. 'How cold you must be! Come in and get dry by the fire. This gentleman is Valentin. He has brought the most charming little buttons and brooches to show me. You must help me choose or I shall take them all.'

The buttons were the prettiest things. Tiny flowers, carved of wood, only so delicate you might have taken them for real. I remember looking at his hands then, and marvelling at the power of them, such masculine hands, how they could have made something so fine. He gave me a little primrose. 'A pretty thing,' he said, 'for a pretty lady'. I blushed then but he only smiled, flashing gold in his teeth. I still have that button. I keep it pinned under my skirts now, hidden, so no one can take it from me. I will take it to my grave.

And so I made poor Emily tell me everything. He was from a proud gypsy race, the Roma, his people lived in Dulwich for the winter, on the south side of the river, where they kept to themselves, except to sell pegs or brushes, or receive ladies at the camp to have their fortunes told. He had been coming to the shop to sell gypsy wares for a year or two, and Emily found him perfectly charming, and honest in their dealings. And where most of his kind did not care to mix – or even talk – with the *gadje*, as they called us, he liked to speak with whom he chose, and to do as he pleased. His mother's side had *gadje* blood, he had said, and when he found the girl he loved, he would marry her whether she was Romani or *gadje*, or she

65

came from the moon. My heart leaped at that. I pinned the button to my breast and swore I would never dress without it. But I did not tell Emily that, yet.

Only, of course, she noticed, by and by. 'Why, but I never see you without that button on your dress, Miss Tabitha,' she said. 'You must be uncommonly fond of it.' I blushed at that, for I had been thinking of him not a moment before and it was as if she had read my mind. 'Oh!' said she. 'Perhaps it is not just the button you have taken a fancy to!' At that I flushed still redder and hid; she laughed at me, and pulled my hands away to look at my hot face, her eyes twinkling.

And in spite of my blushing, or the danger of it, I had been hoping he would be there every Tuesday morning, although I had not seen him the last two. If I had known when else he might have called at the shop I would have changed my routine – but I did not, and so I thought it best to keep my habits just the same, as Tuesday was the day I had seen him first. The week seemed to crawl by before Tuesday came round again. And then, as if God was rewarding my patience, there he was. I forget what he was selling, embroidery, perhaps, or some such thing – I paid no attention to it but looked only at him, and tried with all my might not to blush. He told me he had been thinking of me – oh! the thrill of that! – and when he looked at me, his dark eyes seemed to say a thousand secret things.

Well, after that we met every Tuesday morning, first thing, before the shop opened. Emily would give us a little privacy to talk and hold hands, and before very long I knew that if I could not be with Valentin all my life, I had better not live at all. Indeed, already it was a fearful torment to wait a week before I could see him again – I would pine for him so dreadfully that it made me feel quite ill. And evidently he felt the same agony, for he started to write me letters between one visit and the next, and send them to Emily's shop, so as to keep our secret, and she would bring them to the back door at Cavendish Square so that I would not have to suffer a moment's waiting, she said. She was *so* very dear to me then.

I confided in her one day, telling her how I loved Valentin with all my heart and soul, and that I wanted to marry him, but I knew not what to do, for my parents would sooner lock me in the Tower than countenance the match. She looked at me so very sadly then, and said that for all my wealth and comfort she did not envy me for I was bound by it. The poor, she said, at least, were free. I thought about this again and again – those words rang around my head. *The poor, at least, were free.* And I began to envy their freedom. Although Valentin was not so very poor – indeed, he told me, he wanted for nothing at all. But surely, said Emily, when next we met, I would not give up the privilege and comfort of my position for love! Surely not! And I knew the answer to that question before she had come to the end of it – yes, I would! I would. I would give up anything for my love.

'Well, then, surely you may marry whomsoever you choose,' she said.

It was that very afternoon that Mama told me I was to stay with the Dents, in Wiltshire. For two weeks! How was I to bear it? And just three days after that, as I sat at another dinner in the Dent family's gloomy dining hall, looking at the stuffed heads of wild things, I knew that Emily was right. I knew I must break the shackles of my family's wishes and be free.

I know that I was rude to leave the Dent house in the way

that I did it. I would have done better to bide my time a little and depart with good grace. But I could not help myself. I am ruled by my heart, and I am not sorry for it. I will follow my foolish heart to the grave.

*

My poor dear Mama never did a single thing just as she pleased. Her every day was prescribed, a never-ending round of visits, and teas, and seasonal things. Father told her what to do sometimes from the privacy of his club, though really he did not give a fig. And even the servants: although it seemed that Mama was giving them the orders, in fact she was not. 'Will my lady take tea in the upstairs drawing room now?'; 'Will my lady take a turn around the park this afternoon?' These were little hands on her back, pushing her in this or that direction: Mama did nothing of her own volition. If no one had come I think she would have sat in her chair until she expired from lack of sustenance. She had no free spirit. When she went out shopping it was to buy something somebody had told her she should have, in whichever colour she had been advised was most in fashion. When she visited the theatre it was to take in whatever show was the new sensation, where she would laugh when everybody else did, admire the talent that was that week's toast of the town. She drove Cook up the wall with *à la mode* French cuisine, the *pommes à la Condé*, the *riz de veau aux tomates*, where before our guests had done with saddle of mutton or boiled custards.

Rose, the fortune-teller, was another of these fancies. She had already read fortunes at Baroness Chorley's house, at a gathering earlier that month, and that was enough for Mama. The year before we had hosted a seance after Baroness Chorley had thrown one. Thrown one? Is that the right word for it? I expect not. It makes it sound like a party. At any rate, I had come – dare I say it? – to despise my mother, just a little, for her superficiality, and more and more I had found myself gazing through the drawing-room windows, out over Cavendish Square, yet a thousand miles away.

It was Emily who hatched the plan. Or, rather, it was she who refined it, made it foolproof. I was ready to steal from the house in the dead of night with only a bag to my name and go to him at Dulwich. I had done it in my dreams, gone over and over it until I could bear it no longer, the waking in Cavendish Square without him, and I knew that I should have to escape whatever might become of me. I had told him what was in my heart and he had said come to him before I died of waiting, before the camp moved for the summer, and so I had set a date, and packed my little bag, and hidden it at the back of my armoire, and at last I told Emily.

Emily had said nothing at first, but only looked awhile at me, and then she said, would my dear parents not begin the search for me the very next morning, when my bed was found empty? And did I not think that it would give me a very short start and had I better not steal a longer march on them, perhaps? And when I thought of what she said it seemed my plan grew cracks and fell apart inside my head. Moreover, she said, was there not the chance I might be seen at Dulwich? And, though it was obviously not very important for a free spirit, would I not like a few more clothes and comforts than I might take with me in one bag? Well, I said, it seemed that she was right. Emily was so very clever. But I did not know how I might do it any differently.

She leaned her chin in her hand upon the counter and was quiet for several long moments. Then she got up and walked the length of the shop – slowly, deliberately, as if she went deeper in thought with every step – and bolted the door, turning the sign over to read *Closed*. When she returned to the counter her eyes were shining, lit up quite brilliantly with an idea. She was *so very* clever, my poor, dear Emily. Perhaps, she said, the key was not in leaving under cover of darkness, in secret, risking discovery, but in broad daylight, with your parents' blessing. It will never happen, I told her. Not with him, she said. You cannot leave with him. Only you might leave with me.

'Wait a little longer', she said. 'The gypsies will be gone in another week. And then we might set off upon a little tour – a trip to the seaside, say. And, once we are far from London, you could meet Valentin not at Dulwich, but far away somewhere: in Gravesend, say, or Herne Bay and go on with him wherever the road takes you.'

Wherever the road takes us! What an enchanting thought that was.

'By the time I return, and tell them that you have gone,' she said, 'you will be over the hills and far away.'

By the time she returned I would be jumping the broomstick with my true love. 'Tell them that,' I said, 'and tell them not to look for me, for I shall never come back. By the time you return, I shall be a gypsy woman. I shall roast hedgehogs on the camp fire, and polish my little painted wagon, shine every inch of it. I shall sing gypsy songs and dance wild gypsy dances, and I shall learn to speak Romani, and if ever you see me again my skin will be so brown from the sun that you will not know me. People will watch me pass proudly through their towns atop the painted steps of my wagon and wonder where this proud gypsy girl came from and they will never know that I was once a pale girl in a grand house in Cavendish Square. Why, I will be a thousand miles from it!'

'Yes,' said my dear Emily, 'yes indeed. But first must come the particulars.' She was so practical, and so very clever. By the very next day we had hatched a plan. I was to ask Mama for permission to visit Lady Jocelyn, in St Leonards, near Hastings – and to take Emily with me. Of course she would consent to it. Lady Frances Jocelyn had been one of Mama's best dinner guests only the month before – even Papa had dragged himself away from his club that evening – and she had invited me to stay at her seaside home during the summer, which Mama had been urging me to do every day since. We would take the train from London Bridge station, south, to Beckenham, as Mama supposed, where we would stop for a few days to visit Emily's dear mother, whom Emily said she had not seen for almost a year. From there, we told her, we would rejoin the Chatham and Dover railway at Croydon, and so on to St Leonards and Hastings.

Of course we were never to take the train to Beckenham. To this very day I do not know if Emily's mother truly lives in Beckenham, or Sydenham, or anywhere at all. It was a way of buying a little time, a day or two before we were expected at Hastings and alarms were raised. Because, you see, we were never to arrive.

We were to set off in another direction altogether, east,

following the river Thames, past Greenwich, and Woolwich, to Gravesend. And there, at the encampment by the coast road, would be Valentin, waiting for me. He wrote to me – we did not risk talking at the shop – telling me what we would do then, declaring his love. Emily and I would spend the night in his sister's wagon while he stoked the fire and talked with the men, and the next morning we would marry, he and I, beneath the blue summer sky, with all the family to witness it, he in his best clothes and I with daisies in my hair. And then we would climb aboard our new wagon and roll away down the road with the Roma. And Emily would return to London to break the news to my poor mama that I had eloped. Somewhere between Croydon and Lewes, as she slept: she had woken to find me gone from the train, bags and all, quite without warning or trace, save for a farewell note in my own rather untidy hand:

My dear Emily,

It is with regret that I abandon you in this way. If there were another I should never have done such a thing, for you have been very dear to me. But, indeed, there is not – I must follow my heart, and no one, not even you, my sweet friend, must pursue me, and so I must leave you in secret. I have gone with my love, the man I would give my life to, without whom I shall surely wither and die. Be happy for me, if you can. Ask my mother and father to forgive me, and never to look for me, for I am blown away on the wind.

With my greatest affection
Tabitha

We went out the very next evening to celebrate. Valentin wore a fine suit, and bought us a French dinner at Jaquet's. And then afterwards, though he said it was no place for ladies, he took us to the famous – or, rather, infamous – Argyll Rooms. It was I who begged to go: I had heard such talk of it, and read so many bad things about it in the paper. Why did I want to go to the Argyll Rooms, of all the places on earth? he asked me. 'Let us just say I am curious,' I told him, 'and I have a head for adventure.'

Did I know it was a haunt of fallen women and unlikely characters? 'Why, we may as well take a stroll down the Haymarket after the clock has struck twelve,' he said.

'We may as well, then,' said I. 'For I would follow you anywhere. To the ends of the earth.'

He laughed then, and took my hand. 'Did you hear, Emily?' he said. 'She will follow me to the ends of the earth.'

*

Lady Jocelyn obliged us with an invitation to visit Hastings in the first week of July. It was three weeks before we left: three interminable weeks of waiting, and longing, and dreaming of my love. Could we not just go now? I asked Emily, as the second week began. Must I wait? 'Of course you must,' she said, rather sternly. 'You must be patient. Everyone must believe that we truly are to stay with Lady Jocelyn. Everything must seem real.' She was right, of course.

The plan went without a hitch. Mama never suspected a thing. When she saw that I was wearing my old grey poplin dress, the one I used to wear for Sunday school, she only said,

'Whatever are you wearing that old thing for, my dear? It is very plain. Do you think it good enough to arrive in at Lady Jocelyn's house?' I told her it was comfortable for travelling in, and that we should not be arriving at Lady Jocelyn's house today at any rate, and reminded her that we were to visit Emily's mother in Beckenham first, to which she said, 'Oh, yes, of course. Well, I am sure it is good enough for Beckenham.' And when I held her just a little too tight as I said goodbye – for I knew that it was the last time I would see her – she only laughed in her silly way and said, 'Goodness me Tabitha, how you are crushing my poor ribs! You will not be gone for very long, dear. Do not fret so, I shall see you back again soon enough.'

I wanted to tell her then – 'No, Mother! No, you shall never see me again! Not while there is life in my body you shall not.'

But I only smiled, a little sadly, at her, turned my back and alighted the carriage steps. And I rolled out of Cavendish Square, casting off my old life like a worn-out skin.

*

We went east, threading our way through the London traffic, towards London Bridge. Mama had wanted to come and see us off: somehow I had managed to dissuade her, with Emily's help – railway stations were noisy, vexatious places, I reminded her. She herself hated farewells, and it would be an uncomfortable squeeze in the carriage with all the cases. I could not have faced it: the journey, with her twittering in my ear, asking the same questions over again, dispensing the same cautions, and instructions, and messages for Lady Jocelyn, and, as much as

I was glad to be leaving Cavendish Square behind I could not have borne another moment of deceiving her.

We waved the coachman away as soon as a porter had our cases, fearing a little that he might see us on to the Beckenham train, but by the time they were loaded on to the trolley, and we were heading to the ticket office, he was out of sight. Before we knew it we were on the Greenwich line train for Gravesend, the whistle was blowing and it was pulling away from the platform. With eagle eyes Emily raked the crowd outside until we were out of the station. Only then did she sit back and breathe a tiny sigh of relief.

The countryside rattled past us, fields of yellow and green, spring lambs gambolling, country folk haymaking, living out their lives of rural charm and simplicity. We spoke barely a word. Looking back over it, I wonder what Emily was thinking: if she knew, then, or if she was only sad at the prospect of our parting.

If she was sad I was insensitive to it. I could think only of my love, every moment bringing me nearer to him, every mile of track passing beneath the churning engine, falling behind us, closing the distance. And I spared not a thought for her feelings.

*

Gravesend is not far, just about an hour from London. Before I knew it we were pulling into the station, the whistle was blowing, and we had to leap from our daydreams to our feet and have our bags taken down from the train. And though no one looks twice at a girl in a grey poplin dress, I felt I was being watched by someone I could not see. When I looked into the carriage windows the passengers were reading the papers, or gazing at their fingernails. Only one or two seemed to observe us, and only in a casual way, as if they had nothing better to look at. People bustled around us on the platform, and away to their waiting carriages, and the whistle blew again, and the train pulled out of the station and was gone in a great cloud of smoke. And then there was only Emily, and I, and the porter, asking, 'Where to, ladies?' and the birds singing in the trees.

The driver of the carriage we took was not happy at first to leave us at the side of the coast road. I expected he had heard about the gypsy camp there. People who do not know about the Roma think of them as thieves and vagabonds: perhaps he thought we would be in some danger. Only we gave him half a crown, and he seemed much better about it then. Once he had driven away we picked up our bags and started down the lane. It was quiet. I remember thinking that perhaps we should have to walk further than I had thought to the camp. And my arms were starting to ache after just a few yards, and I was wondering how I would manage, when we rounded the hedgerow and there, across the field, was a lone painted wagon. And before it a fire, with a pot boiling, and, stirring the pot, my beloved, my Valentin. I dropped my bags and ran across the field to him, shouting his name. He looked up, surprised, and then a smile broke across his handsome face, teeth flashing gold and white against his brown skin and he swept me into his arms.

*

76

His family had had to go on without him, he said, as we sat about the fire, eating rabbit stew. The rain in Essex had made for an early harvest so they had been obliged to go straight to their seasonal work in the market gardens, around Rush Green. His sisters had been sorry that they were to miss my arrival, but we would follow them in the morning, and I would meet the family. And then, too, we would ask the bandoleer to marry us, just as we had planned before.

Emily was quiet. I do believe she was doubtful suddenly; now I think back upon it I am not sure of what, for it is all so complicated. And now, after all, it does not matter. But then, I thought – conceitedly, I suppose – that she was concerned at being party to my escape, at how things would go on from here, how I would fare without my fine things and my family, for I heard her say as much to Valentin later. I woke suddenly, in the middle of the night, and it was black as tar inside the wagon – only a flickering light came through the curtain, and I could hear the crackle of a fire and low voices. Emily had risen from the bed and was outside with Valentin. I saw them sitting before the fire, their backs towards me. Something stopped me calling to them: they looked deep in conversation, their heads together, almost touching, and their voices were an urgent murmur. I did not mean to listen but I caught his words: 'Do not fret so, my dear,' he said. 'Nothing can go wrong.'

And then she replied, 'I know, indeed, but my conscience pricks me all the same, just a little.'

And then they were quiet, looking at the fire, and I felt somewhat ashamed for spying on them, and dropped down below the window, but I listened, all the same, for I knew they were talking about me. I heard the rustling of her skirts, a stirring of the fire – and then his voice again, though I did not understand what he meant: 'Does it prick you now, my dear?' he said.

'No indeed,' said she, with a little gasp, as if he had hurt her, and then there was more quiet, only the rustle of the trees and the sighing of the wind in the treetops.

*

The next morning the fire was out and Emily was inside the wagon, and I wondered if I had dreamed it, only Miss Emily was tucked in a blanket on the floor, and I knew she had been out of the bed. She looked so small and fragile, lying there, and I felt so sorry, for a thrill was stirring in my belly, the thrill of knowing that today was to be my first upon the open road with my true love. And I felt sad for Emily that she did not know love, and wished for her to find it one day – though I wondered if that would ever be, for after all she was a little plain, and then I thought this notion unkind, and felt all the sorrier, and before I knew it I had reached out my hand to touch her sleeping face, and she opened her eyes and looked at me.

'Good morning, Tabitha,' she said. 'Did you sleep peacefully?'

'I did, thank you, my dear friend,' I told her. She smiled at that, and closed her eyes again.

'Good luck to you, Tabitha,' she said.

*

Later, Valentin took her to the train on the back of his horse. She covered her head, so as not to be recognized, should anyone come asking after us. And, curiously, she was not so very plain suddenly, as he swung her up to sit behind him. The bones of her face, framed by the scarf, seemed a little exotic, her eyes darker. They looked like a Romani couple, sitting up together on that horse, and I felt a twinge of envy that came out of nowhere and stung me like a poisoned dart.

But I forgot it once he came back alone. No one had seen them. And now there was only him and I. We packed up our things with the warm sunshine on our backs. It was as I folded my night things that I found the letter – the one that Emily was to show Mama, saying I had eloped from the train. It worried me, just for a moment – for it seemed a bad start to my new life, this mistake, but then I thought – no matter! Emily will manage without it. And I tore it into pieces and tossed them into the fire. Valentin hitched up the horse to the wagon, and kicked over the ashes, and we rolled out of that field and were gone.

Report made this 5th July 1860 by Sgt Robert Duff of the Great Marlborough St police office

This morning I have been called to the house of the Quayle family at number 27 Cavendish Square to investigate the kidnapping of Miss Tabitha Quayle, second daughter of Lord and Lady Quayle. On arrival I was shown upstairs to Lady Margaret Quayle's own rooms, where I encountered her much distressed and quite incoherent. I enquired after the whereabouts of Lord Quayle only to be told by the butler – one Mr Thomas – that his lordship was taking luncheon at his club and had not yet been told the dreadful news, though he had been called for and was expected back soon. Mr Thomas then directed me to the only witness, one Emily Budd, and took Lady Quayle from the room to spare her further distress while I interviewed Miss Budd. Miss Budd was somewhat distressed herself, but recovered bravely enough to tell me what had happened. Early that morning, she told me, she and Miss Tabitha had set out for the station at Beckenham to catch a train for the coast. A carriage from the town had come to pick them up, from her mother's house, where they had stayed the two nights previous. They had been in the carriage not ten minutes when it stopped and two men got in. She could not remember where it stopped, exactly. Indeed she looked bewildered when I asked her and said, no, she was not sure at all, did it matter? – and when I explained to her that any detail at all might be helpful to police enquiries she said she was very sorry but she did not know. She remembered only their brutish faces and their heavy hands. Indeed, she said, she saw them every time she closed her eyes, and was sure she would see them in her nightmares that very night.

At this point I was obliged to stop the questioning to allow the witness to collect herself. When she had recovered she gave a detailed description of the two men. Both, she said, were between thirty-five and forty years of age, heavy-set, swarthy and bearded, with large, rough workmen's hands. One had a scar across his left cheek and the other was quite fat; his front teeth were missing. She told me that she was fearful as soon as she saw them, for they looked the criminal type.

'Are you Miss Tabitha Quayle?' one of them had asked, and when Miss Tabitha answered yes, they had laughed, and knocked on the roof for the driver to move on again. By then, said Miss Budd, she and Miss Tabitha had realized they were not going to the station at all. Indeed, all they could see from the window was trees and fields, though, again, she could remember nothing more particular about the landscape that might have helped to place them.

The men let Miss Budd out some two miles down the road, telling her to go back to her master's house – evidently mistaking her for a servant – and tell them that Miss Tabitha was taken and that a ransom demand would follow.

The witness has clearly suffered a trauma which may explain her somewhat uneven memory of events. She has begged me not to visit her mother, who did not see the carriage, the driver, or the two men, knows nothing of this incident and will likely take ill with the shock of it. I propose that we enquire at Beckenham after the local carriages, and post Wanted bills around the area, with a description of these two fellows. Aside from this there is very little to be done, at least until a ransom demand is made.

Chapter Five

Rose

Miss Tabitha taken? How? Emily lowers her red eyes and lets out a silent sob into her tortured handkerchief. 'It was the coachman,' she says. 'We ordered a carriage to take us from Mother's house to Croydon, to join the train to Hastings. And we had been driving awhile when the carriage stopped, and, supposing we had reached the station, we were preparing to climb down when two fellows got in, one by each door.'

Her face creases at the memory of it. Lady Quayle shudders. Emily dabs at her eyes.

'Our first thought,' she whimpers, 'was how very ungentle-manly they were – for they quite blocked our exit – and then we realized that they meant to do it, and for a moment we were very confused. "Is this the station?" said Tabitha, but the men only smiled, in an odd way, as if they had not understood. We thought perhaps they were foreign fellows, only then one of them said, "Are you Miss Tabitha Quayle?" – and oh! If only she had told him no, she might be here now! But she said, "I am," and at that he laughed and said, "Very good!" and the carriage started off again.'

'My poor dear,' sobs Lady Quayle. She looks as if she will faint. Emily leans forward and clasps her hand.

'My lady,' I say, 'must you put yourself through this? Perhaps you would be better to take a tonic and try to have a little rest.'

'Indeed,' she says. 'I cannot bear to hear it over again. My poor, poor dear. What is to become of her?'

'I will come to you later,' I tell her. 'After I hear Emily out.' We call for the butler, who escorts her away for a little brandy-and-water. I turn my full attention on Emily. 'Tell me what happened next,' I say.

After a while of driving, she told me, they realized that they must have missed the station, and asked the men to let them aside to speak to the coachman. But the men had only laughed at this, and when Tabitha had banged on the carriage roof to get the driver's attention they had laughed harder still. Emily, of course, by then had realized what was happening, and knew it was hopeless to speak to the driver anyhow. 'Where are you taking us?' she had asked them then. 'You, little miss, are going back to your Mistress's family,' they said. 'Tell them we have Miss Tabitha. And tell them we will send a ransom demand after you.'

I have a thousand questions for poor Emily. They seem to circle slowly in a tangled ring around the room. Something is not right.

'And has it come, this ransom demand?' I ask her. She looks at me strangely then. All the sadness and despair seem to have left her face. Her hands have stopped worrying; they lie still in her lap.

'Why no,' she says. 'I do not believe it has. I myself arrived only late this morning.'

'I wonder why they did not ask you to deliver it,' I say.

'Well,' she replies, 'who knows? Or, indeed, cares? I want only the safe return of my dear friend.' She clasps her hands then, distractedly across her heart, and looks at me with wide, empty eyes.

'Of course you do,' I tell her.

'I suppose,' says she, twisting a tight little knot in the corner of her handkerchief, 'that perhaps they might send this ransom demand after me so Lord and Lady Quayle would be sure that it was genuine.'

'How so?'

'Well, I mean, to show that I had no hand in writing it.'

'And why on earth would they suppose that Lord and Lady Quayle should think such a thing?'

'They might have thought that it would look strange if I arrived with a ransom letter in my pocket,' she says. 'Do you not think it would?'

'I have not given it a thought,' I tell her.

Her eyes do not blink. A muscle twitches in her cheek.

'Do you think it would have looked strange?' I ask her. 'If you had arrived with a ransom note in your pocket?'

She looks angry then, for a second, it comes like a flash of lightning across her face: if I had blinked I might have missed it. And suddenly Miss Emily Mouse's eyes look hard – though she tries to cover it with the look of affronted innocence.

*

My grandmother told me, when I was just a tiny thing and started to look at my own hand, 'Don't take this piece and that,' she said, 'and write the *Evening News* with it.' I can see her, sat at the table, a deck of cards in one hand, her pipe in the other, the lamplight wavering on the cloth. 'You will be wrong, most likely,' she said. 'You will be making five from two and two. It is not our business to write the story, only to read the signs. And whatever is written will unfold by itself.'

And what have I done but that? In my mind I had Miss Emily Mouse murdered, and here she is alive and well, for one thing. And up to something crooked, it seems. And as for Miss Tabitha, who knows where she might be? I have been wrong. I have been reading this hand and that hand, and writing the *Evening News* – not only the story, but all the characters in it.

I hear old Hannah Smith's voice clear in my ear.

Whatever is written will unfold by itself.

*

They had left Emily at the side of the road somewhere near Croydon, the story went, and had driven away with poor Miss Tabitha to Heaven only knows where. The coachman had disappeared altogether – indeed, the police reported that the carriage company had no record of any carriage ordered for the journey to the station, though Emily swore that they had left instructions to that effect at the coach office. No one troubled Emily's poor dear mother with the news: there would have been nothing she could tell the police that might have helped with their enquiries, and she was a frail woman, with a weak heart, who had never been the same since her husband had done away with himself. She had had her share of bad news, said Emily, enough to sink a ship, indeed, and she might simply drop down dead with the shock. Best to leave her alone. And so they did. And nothing more was done about anything else besides, for the moment.

The police and the household of twenty-seven Cavendish Square wait in a state of awful suspense, like pickled specimens in jars.

*

And then, on Saturday, a note comes. It is dropped through the letterbox at twenty-seven Cavendish Square by an unseen hand. It smells of tobacco, and axle grease, and this is what it says:

> *Lord Quayle –*
>
>   *We have your daughter. If you want to see her alive again you must deliver the sum of five thousand pounds to the crossroads by Blackheath Gate on the fourteenth of July, a week hence, at nine o'clock in the evening. You must send one servant, unarmed, alone. Once it is done we shall tell you where to find her. If you fail we will send you back your daughter's fingers, one by one, until you comply.*
>
>   *See it done.*

'What do you make of it, Rose?' says Lady Quayle, searching my face with those wide, childish eyes that make me want to slap her, or shake her a little.

What do I make of it? It seems perfectly straightforward to me. I wonder what part of it my lady is having difficulty deciphering. 'Well, Lady Quayle,' I begin, 'it is a most upsetting thing to read. These kidnappers are clearly ruthless men, and not to be trifled with.'

'That is just what Emily said,' she tells me. 'Those were her very words, indeed! Not to be trifled with.' Here, her voice shakes a little. She stops to compose herself.

'So you have shown this to Emily?' I ask her.

'Oh, yes, I have kept Emily up with everything. The dear creature comes by every morning on her way to the shop, just to look in on me, and to see if there is any news. She is so very worried, and guilty.'

'Guilty, my lady?'

'Yes, well, she feels it is all her fault, you see. She feels that if they had not been stopping off in Beckenham to visit her mother none of this would have happened.'

'I think she might take a crumb of comfort from knowing that these are plainly professional men, my lady, who were set upon snatching Tabitha' – here Lady Quayle lets out a delicate sob – 'and thoroughly smart about it: they would likely have tracked her down whether she had been visiting Emily's mother or not,' I tell her. 'Indeed, one might have said something was always going to happen.' Lady Quayle dabs at her eyes again, looking comforted and confused in equal parts. 'The thing that baffles me,' I continue, 'is how they knew where she would be at all. Had she told anybody she was to visit the coast?'

My lady looks sheepish. 'I did mention it to a few people at dinner last week,' she says. 'And perhaps I have broadcast it a little here and there on my rounds.' She hangs her head. 'I had no idea it was doing any harm. I was so pleased for her, you see, to be visiting Lady Jocelyn. She is such a very . . . *exciting* person – at the centre of fashionable society, you know – and her daughters would be such ideal friends for Tabitha: just exactly the sort of girls I want her to keep company with . . .'

She does not finish her sentence but I know what she wants to say: rather than someone like Emily.

'Has Lord Quayle seen the letter?' I ask her. For it occurs to me that it is addressed to him, and him alone, and yet here is Lady Quayle showing it about – in spite of the awful distress it causes her – as if it were a Christmas card: I expect her to put it on the mantel, but she tucks it back into a drawer in her writing desk.

'He has seen it. But he will say nothing more than that he will decide in due course the best thing to be done!' she wails, turning her tear-stained face to me. 'And he will hear no more talk of it. I fear he has forgotten it already, for he has been at his club every waking hour since!' She stops to draw a ragged breath, worn out from sobbing and carrying on.

'Oh, Rose,' she cries, chest heaving, but real wet tears also on her witless cheeks, 'Rose, I am in such depths of despair! What is to become of my beautiful, gentle girl?' She throws herself down then, upon the nearest chair, fair soaking the upholstery with her sorry tears.

Hmm. We shall see about 'gentle girl'. I remember Tabitha's palm, and her cold eyes, like wet stones, and I do not fear for her safety one jot. I can't help but fear rather for that of the person who is keeping her against her will. Although I mustn't make five out of two and two, I tell myself.

'Will you consult the crystal ball, Rose?' asks Lady Quayle, desperation wavering in her voice.

Not the crystal ball, my lady, I think. We may as well consult the birds in the trees.

But we could have a look at the cards.

Cards do not deal with traits of character or matters of the spirit, but only practical things – death, travel, money, marriage. My grandmother was the best reader of cards there has ever been. They suited her, she being a practical woman. And people came back to her again and again because she was always right, and her advice was never vague, or mysterious, but hit the nail square on the head.

She would spread them out in complex patterns across the tabletop and interpret their message according to the order they were set down, whether they lay this way or that, the groups they fell into. She tried to teach me but I never had her talent for it. In the end I mastered only one spread, laid out like the four points of the compass, and she was satisfied enough with that to give me the deck.

I can see her when I close my eyes: in shadow, her hands moving over these very cards, gold shining on her knarled fingers. She never let me try to read her fortune. I do not know if she read it herself.

*

Lady Quayle watches intently as I lay out the spread. The Queen of Diamonds at the centre, to represent her, with her dark eyes and her grey hair. Then the rest around it, in four groups: what it is in her mind, what does she step on, what is in front of her, what is behind. There is nothing much in the first group: nothing I don't know about. The Queen of Clubs, which she steps on, is Miss Emily. In front of her, three Kings, representing authority, court perhaps, the law. And two black sevens, for sorrow and tears, though I don't tell her as much. Behind her, the money card, ten of diamonds, and the seven, reversed.

'Someone who deceives you. Someone close.'

'Deceives me?' she says, her face a picture of confusion. 'Who could want to deceive me? And why?' She worries at this question for as long as she can manage, staring into a spot in front of the wallpaper, with its pattern as crowded yet static as the inside of her head. When she looks blankly back at me I want to take her by the shoulders and shake her. *A draper's shop girl, my lady! And I myself! And likely your staff, and your husband as well!* And I feel just a little guilty, for she is such a very easy target.

And then her face lights up with some idea come upon her, and for an instant I imagine she has seen through me, and knows everything, but this notion dissolves as quickly as it appears.

'Do you suppose it could be Cook?' says she. 'Only I wonder sometimes, when I look at the butcher's bill, which gets bigger every month, how it is that we seem to eat such a great deal of tongue. To look at it one would imagine we dined on fillet steaks and best end of neck every day.'

'Well, my lady,' I begin, searching for the words to tell her – It is Emily, plain Emily Mouse, who is hiding something! – and then I see that little square paw upon the cloth again, and I remember what was marked on her palm: that little cross on the Saturnian line, the grille on the Mount of Mars, the Cerebral line sloping down towards the wrist, with another cross at its end that matches the first.

Fearful, violent death. Clear as a grinning skull.

Let it come upon her under its own steam. By some unknown circumstance. By chance, or accident, or carelessness. But not with my pennyworth. I want no part in dealing Emily's fate.

'Well, my lady,' I say, 'these cards say nothing about the

cook. Or indeed, any steaks, or neck, or tongue. But I have a notion you might keep one eye upon the footman.'

*

'How many fingers do you suppose they will have to send?' says Lillie, tucking into a fat boned bloater, with boiled potatoes.

'You are a callous, shameful creature,' I tell her. 'And you have butter running down your chin.'

'Well?' she says.

'I am not sure there will be any fingers at all. Indeed, the more I think about it, the more certain I am that there will not.' I could swear Lillie looks disappointed. 'After all, I have read Miss Tabitha Quayle's palm myself and it says nothing of any severed parts.'

'Was there anything in it about a kidnapping?' says Lillie.

'There was an unexpected journey.' I trace along Tabitha's lines again in my mind, trying to remember them. There was a little dark spot on the heart line. 'And an unlikely man.'

*

On Wednesday morning I visit Emily's shop, which stands at the corner of Orchard and Somerset Street, the north side of Oxford Street, towards Marble Arch. From across the road I can make her out, bustling about inside, making ready for the day. I stop by the window to look before I go in. There she is, tweaking a display of lace, shaking out the tassels on a satin shawl, with her head to one side, like a beady little bird. The bell rings as I step across the mat. She looks up.

91

Just the faintest trace of – what? alarm? – goes across her face, like a shadow, then she smiles and says what a pleasant surprise it is to see me there, and that she hopes the shop is to my liking. I tell her it is charming, and what a lovely display of silk handkerchiefs. Might she help me with some ribbon and thread? I need a plain black one for an old hat and some grey darning wool.

'Tell me, Emily my dear,' I say, as she busies about behind the counter, 'what news of Tabitha? I am loath to distress poor Lady Quayle by asking her every day. Have the police progressed with their enquiries?'

'Oh, no,' she says, over her shoulder. 'To our great consternation there seems to be no progress whatsoever.'

'None at all, indeed? Poor Lady Quayle must be beside herself with worry,' I muse.

'Oh, my poor dear Tabitha!' cries Emily, suddenly, clutching a card of horn buttons to her breast. 'When I think of her, wherever she is, trapped, and alone, frightened out of her wits, no doubt, I simply cannot bear it.' These are strong words for Emily. Indeed, I have not heard her say so many words at once before. And then she turns on me such a look of abject despair that if I were a valiant gentleman I would have set forth that very instant to scour the countryside until I found her lost friend or fell down dead in the attempt. I offer her my commiserations and hope that this dreadful business will be resolved very soon. Then I pay for my ribbon and thread, thank her for her kind service and wish her good day.

On my way out my eye falls on a little tray of buttons: tiny flowers, carved in wood. Just like the gypsies on Dulwich Common used to make.

Back at Mrs Bunion's I take out the letter I received the very first thing that morning – brought by the poor footman, up with the lark – to read it again, in case I had imagined its contents.

My dear Rose,

Some good news at last. Lord Quayle has agreed to the demands of the ransom note. He is making the arrangements as I write this. Please come to advise me as soon as you are able.

Thanking you in advance, my good dear,

Margaret, Lady Quayle

And as I tuck it back into the drawer I wonder how it is that she has not told Emily as yet. Poor dear Emily, who is so very worried.

*

'What good news it is, my lady,' I tell her, noting how the weight seems already lifted from her shoulders, though her daughter is absent still.

'Is it not, my dear! We are so very much relieved.'

'I expect Emily is much relieved as well.'

'Oh, Emily was overjoyed, indeed. She tried to temper it, to be cautious, bless her heart, for Tabitha is not yet out of the woods, but I could see a little sparkle returning to her eye.'

'And when did you tell her the news?'

'Well, as soon as I heard, of course. I could not keep it from her for an instant, not when she is so very worried.'

And so it seems the grand Quayle family of Cavendish Square are to bend to the will of their tormentors and deliver five thousand pounds – at a junction of the Kent Road, near Deptford, where the countryside begins – on Saturday next, at dusk. Lord Quayle will take it there himself. And I can't say as I blame him. He will go alone, and unarmed, just as the note instructs, then withdraw to wait at the Commercial Docks where his daughter will be delivered: at the entrance between Randall's-rents and the Dog-and-Duck-stairs. He is making a most admirable leap of faith but then what choice does he have? Only that he might wait and see how ruthless these unseen captors truly are. And how many fingers his daughter is worth.

Saturday comes. I imagine Lord Quayle pacing his rooms at Cavendish Square, wearing away the carpet – but Lady Quayle tells me that afternoon that he has enjoyed a good luncheon of chops at his club, and is taking a nap upstairs before setting out. Darkness is falling as I leave her. I hear him call for his man as I slide down the back stairs. Instead of turning off Oxford Street, down to Soho, I keep going east.

*

Deptford is an unremarkable spot. It is well chosen by Miss Tabitha's abductors, for it is quiet at night and concealed: the road bends away to the south and the east not fifty yards from the junction, so anyone coming thence will be heard before they are seen. I arrive on foot, across the fields. When I take my place in a broom thicket by the crossroads it is a quarter to nine. I fancy I hear rustling in the woods across the way. But it is night, and many things may be rustling in the woods as a matter of course.

After a short wait comes a portly figure through the darkness, carrying a carpet bag, and though I have never had the pleasure of his acquaintance I know that he is Lord Quayle, and not one of his servants, as the ransom note directs. He has borrowed his butler's uniform, which does not fit him properly, and he seems most reluctant to let go of the bag. He stops in the very centre of the junction, clutching it close and looks about him, peering into the shadows, turning his face towards the very spot where I crouch – even as I think that there is no way he could see me, I shrink back further into the bushes and my heart begins to beat harder, pulse thumping up my neck, drumming at my ears. He seems to look right at me through the dark for an age, and then he puts the bag down at the foot of the signpost and he is gone. I try to calm my breath as I wait for whoever will follow.

*

I don't wait for long. First I hear a crackle of twigs in the trees behind me. I freeze every muscle, holding my breath. Then a curse, and a lantern, and a great crashing through the bushes, a hand on my shoulder, and – 'Oh! What is this we have here?' – a great burly officer of the law shining a lantern into my face, with all his fellows bringing up the rear. A rattle of cuffs, and rough hands seize me – and I feel, all at once, in that instant, what a fool I have been, what a sorry fool – and that I am good as hanged already.

This morning I have interviewed a Miss Rose Lee, of the
Buttered Bun coffee house, Soho Square, who was brought in
last night after her capture at Blackheath Gate, in connection
with the recent kidnapping of Lady Tabitha Quayle. She is a
most uncooperative subject.

At first I asked her how it was that she came to be at such
a remote spot at such an hour of the night; the accused reported,
with an insolent smirk, that she was picking blackberries. In
the dark? Yes, she said, in the dark. Did she know how very
suspicious it looked, her being there, I asked her then. She
replied that, yes, she expected it did but that I would have to
do better than suspicious. When I told her that if she continued
in this manner I would lock her back in the cell and continue
the interview tomorrow she said she reckoned she would be
going back in there anyhow. 'It must be all my doing,' she
said. 'There wasn't anybody else there, was there?' I asked her
who she had been expecting to see there.

She was quiet for several minutes. 'Emily,' she said at last,
very calm. Emily who? 'I do not know her family name,' she
said. 'She works in a draper's shop, off Oxford Street.' And what
did she know of Emily? She had read fortunes for them all at
the Quayle house, she told me, at her ladyship's *soirées*. Then
what had led her to suspect this Emily had had a hand in Lady
Tabitha's abduction? She was quiet for a time before she said,
'Something is not right about Emily's story. Ask her yourself.'

We have spoken to Miss Emily Budd already, I told her, and her story seemed watertight enough to me. And, furthermore, it was Miss Budd who had first suggested that *she* might have had a hand in the whole sorry business. Indeed, I said, we have been following your movements from the start. Miss Lee had nothing to say to this, but only hung her head, then shook it, slowly, as if defeated.

I enquired then who else was involved. Again, she paused for a time. 'I do not know,' she told me, by and by. And that was all she would say about it.

I asked her why she had not mentioned Emily in the first place, but rather halfway through the interview, as if she had thought of it only just then – or made it up, indeed. 'I am a Romani,' was her reply. 'We answer to the Kris, or the King, or the bandoleer. And you – you are a *"gadje"* policeman.'

You live in Soho Square, do you not? I asked her. 'Yes, I do,' she said. Apart from your own people? 'What of it?' she replied. I asked her why it was she chose to live in the *'gadje'* city and what business she had here, to which she told me it was none of my concern, and that she was 'up to the gills with stupid questions.'

At that I informed her that she was to be held here and charged with being a party to the abduction of Miss Tabitha Quayle, extortion with resort to personal violence, and intent to harm involving risks to life. Then she was taken back down.

Chapter Six

Rose

Lady Quayle does not take the stand or, indeed, attend my trial. The only witnesses are policemen: it takes no time at all – though the moment's pause the jury foreman takes to compose himself before he speaks his only word seems to last for ever. He looks at me as he might look at dog shit on the paving: what business do I have in his city? And by what right do I imagine I may call at the houses of lords and ladies and bring my sordid hokum into the very rooms where they eat, and entertain grand guests? I know he would like to stick my head upon a spike on Temple Bar, if he could, and I know what he will say – he, and the judge, before he even dons his black cap – and not because I have read it in the cards, or the stars, or my wretched palm: but across their hard faces.

Indeed, I have sworn not to look at my own fortune at all. And every time I am tempted I remember.

Life is like streaky bacon.

I murmur it to myself now, as he pronounces death upon me. Streaky bacon. Life, and death.

And then they take me down again.

*

'You have a visitor,' says the warden at Horsemonger Lane, who is a woman so ugly that it shocks me anew each time I see her. I resolve not to look directly at her again. I feel I may turn to stone. And there behind her is Lillie, grimacing. She brings pickled eggs, and ham, and porter. We sit upon the filthy straw mattress that furnishes my cell.

'So,' says she, and looks at me as if to say something more, something bright and carefree, to lift my spirits – but words seem to fail her and she grasps my hand, her face creasing.

'Don't you dare cry,' I tell her. 'Only get me out of here.'

'How can I?'

'You must tell Lady Quayle that Emily knows something.'

'But she mustn't know we're acquainted! Or we'll both swing for certain.'

'Oh, Lillie!' I scold her. 'We will not! For Heaven's sake, anyone might think you couldn't be bothered.'

'Of course I can,' she says, a little offended.

'Write her an anonymous letter. Put it through her door, after dark. Tell her I am innocent. Tell her Emily knows where her daughter has gone.'

*

Lillie returns that afternoon. As if to prove me wrong in being so faithless she has not only prepared the letter, which she will deliver at nightfall, but has visited Emily's shop to speak to her directly. She found the blinds drawn down and the door closed – but, turning to leave, who should she run smack into

99

but Lady Quayle herself, alighting from her carriage, looking up at the first-floor window, a frown upon her genteel brow.

'Well!' says Lillie. 'I wasn't wearing my ugly brown dress, of course, but I looked sober and Christian enough so I thought it right enough to greet her – "Why, good Lady Quayle!" I said. "What a surprise it is to see you here!" Well, our lady seemed a thousand miles away. Indeed, she looked straight through me at first, before she came to and returned the greeting. "Are you come here?" she says, pointing at the shop. "Oh, yes," says I. "I've come for buttons. I was told it is the very best shop for buttons in the district." – "Indeed it is," says Lady Quayle. "What a pity it is closed." – "Well," says I, "I was thinking the self-same thing. Is it usually shut on a Thursday?" – "No, indeed," says our lady, and she looks up at the windows above the shop front again. "It has been closed since Monday," she says. "I do hope it will be open soon." And that was that! She wishes me good day, hops back into her carriage and off she goes. What do you think of that, Rose? Should I put the letter through her door tonight? Should I watch the shop?'

Poor Lillie. She has had a hard enough life for anyone, but nary a frown has crossed her sweet, cheery face for any of it. Now she wears the despair she has shrugged off with every one of those troubles, and all at once. I cannot bear to see her take on so.

'Oh, Lillie,' I tell her, 'you are a good kind friend, and I am lucky for that. And if Emily is gone, she is gone. I do not know, in truth, what is to be gained if she were found, unless it is with her hands in the ransom purse. Do not fret, my dear, only sit here with me and let us have some more porter. Here's to you, and all the blessings of Providence that heap on your sweet head.'

*

Mrs Bunion comes in the evening. She brings currant buns, and boiled eggs, and bacon.

'What a very ugly thing she is,' she says, as the warden has barely turned her back. 'I'd step on her face as soon as look at her.'

I thank her for the buns, and eggs, and bacon. I want to cry when I see them, all packed into a little box with a napkin. I want to throw myself into Mrs Bunion's arms and cry like a baby. But I do not want to worry her, so I only smile, as best I can, and peel an egg, though I'm not hungry.

'What's it all about, dear?' she asks, as I knew she would. 'I'll wager Miss Lillie Daley has a hand in it.'

'She hasn't, Mrs B. I've got myself here all alone.'

'Dipping pockets, were you?' she says, shaking her head.

'That's about the size of it, Mrs B.'

'Silly girl.' She puts an arm around me and pats my back. 'You eat your egg. You'll be home before you blink.'

*

That night I hear prayers, crazed, cursed prayers, and a terrible howling. Holy Trinity's bells begin to ring for the condemned – twelve plaintive strikes, a hollow song, the very sound of hopelessness – their execution day is tomorrow. Some hour of the night, it seems the darkest, there comes a hum, like growling, growing slowly louder. It's the crowd outside the gates, filling up the street beneath the gallows, and as dawn breaks and the light begins to crawl up the sky, as it must do, they start to shriek and cackle at the day, like wild packs of ragged animals. And I wonder if the condemned are at their barred windows, watching the sun rise, relentless as the tide – the last few grains running through the hourglass – and willing it to stop. Or is it a blessed relief to see it? Do they urge it on faster to escape this creeping torment, inch by inch towards the platform and the noose and the drop, played out by the demented song of the mob outside?

I sit still upon the floor until it is light enough to see the hand I am clutching shut. I haven't looked at it, still: I am frightened of what will be marked upon it. I hear the priest at the next cell door, the drone of a prayer, a shriek, a sob. I take a ragged breath and I uncurl my fist.

Is it possible to feel such hope and joy at such a dreadful prospect, written there upon my palm as plain as india ink? That tiny star, on Luna's mount. Not the gallows, the raging crowd, not the rope.

Death by drowning, it says, clear as black and white! You shall surely suffer death by drowning.

Chapter Seven

Tabitha

We did not catch up with Valentin's family the next day, after all. We awoke, in our little wagon, under a great willow tree, with a soft breeze blowing and the morning sun lighting the branches gold and green. Valentin watered the horse – how good he was with animals! I watched his strong hands on that horse's neck, how he murmured into her ear, and my belly felt a curious thrill: a swooning, aching sensation I can feel even now, as I think of him. When he had stoked the embers and put a pot to boil he turned to me and looked for a long time. Then he took my face in his hands and kissed me once, and then again, full upon the lips, and his chin grazed me as he pushed his tongue between them and ran it across my teeth and inside my mouth as if he were eating a peach. It was wet, and soft, and . . . well, I have not words to describe it – the thrill that gripped my belly from inside, like a serpent uncoiling, running its tail through my guts, between my legs. I had never imagined such a thing before, so forward, and it was shocking, and made me flush bright red with shame.

When Valentin looked at me he did not blink and his eyes

were like burning coals: it seemed as if I knew him but had never seen him before, and though I was abashed, it set my insides on fire. And then I wanted him, and I did not know how, but I wanted him so very badly that it hurt, in a curious, desperate way, urgent as if I would melt, or burst, and I let him take me under the willow tree, running his strong brown hands up under my skirts and gripping me around the waist as he thrust himself into me, right to the spot that ached and itched and stung for him all at once, and all the while he looked at me, with those implacable eyes, hard like those of a wild beast. And then he threw back his head and his body froze and he dug his hands into my hair, and we lay in a tangle of limbs and clothing as if we had been slaughtered under that willow, with the birds singing overhead and the breeze stirring in the leaves.

*

How would I like it, he said, if we did not follow the family on to Rush Green, but went our own sweet way for a while? They would be crossing to Kent in August for the fruit picking; we could join them then. Only he wanted me to himself for just a while longer. I held on to his neck and I kissed his rough cheek. 'I will follow you anywhere,' I told him. 'I will stay with you for ever. I am happy if I never see another soul again.'

And so we stayed there, by the willow tree, that day and the next, and the next, until I lost count of them. We lived on rabbits, and dandelion leaves, and we laid down under that tree again and again, and I imagined how it would be to stay there for ever, forgetting all about the world outside that field, a little more each day until there was nothing left to remember.

*

And then, perhaps ten days after we had arrived, Valentin's gypsy blood rose in his veins – I felt it stir, the wanderlust. Even the horse stamped her feet and shook her mane, as if to say, 'The road is waiting,' and he hitched her to the wagon and we rolled away as the sun began to climb the sky.

He had to go back a little way towards London, he said. There was something he must attend to before we set off alone. But he would not risk taking me there, for what then if I was seen and taken back? Why, he would lose me for ever and he would sooner die. He left me with the wagon in a copse outside Southfleet – to tell the truth, it matters nothing at all where it was, only that it was a dark hillside and a rainy night, and though I had everything I might want inside the wagon, still I was stranded there until he came back for me, and I did not altogether like it, although I had submitted to it. He would be back before the sun set, he said. 'Must you leave me?' I pleaded – but he only shook his head, grave, as if to tell me I must not ask him anything more. It was something he was bound to by his honour, he told me. And that was all that he would say.

He took his clothes, and all his effects, such as they were, with him – if I was found, he said, at least there would be nothing of him left behind to scent the dogs. 'What dogs?' I cried – he alarmed me so. For if they caught him, he said, he would surely hang. You will not hang, I said. 'I will not let it happen! I will tell them everything, how I came here of my own free will, how we are to be married.'

He laughed then, and stroked my face. 'It will not matter,' he said. 'You are a lady and I am a gypsy, and I will surely hang, and then I will never return to you except to haunt you in dreams.'

'Be careful then,' I told him. 'I love you, Valentin, come back to me.'

He laughed then, with his head back, carefree, as if he was challenging the devil himself to stand in his way, and he kissed me hard, and leaped up on the horse's back, and rode off down the road.

*

He was not back before the sun went down. Indeed, there was no sun to go down that day. Rather, a gloom settled over the land, slowly, towards the evening, as if to keep company with the clouds in my head. But I thought of what Valentin had told me: a life on the road is a good life, but hard sometimes. So I tried to be a good Romani wife. I got up from the step, covered my head, and went to forage for sticks in the hedgerow.

Now, foraging for sticks is not the cheery rural pastime it sounds. Most especially it is not in the rain. I was scratched and torn, reaching under the bushes for the dry wood, and stung by nettles. Once a thorny branch snapped back to lash me across the face. I almost gave way to tears. But after perhaps an hour's struggle I had an armful of wood, which I covered with my shawl and carried back to the wagon.

And there my struggles truly began, for I had let the embers of the morning's fire go cold. I had watched Valentin light it, and the one before, and the one before, but now I realized I had been gazing only at him, and not paying attention to what he was doing, not taking it in at all – I might as well have had my eyes tight shut for all the good they did me – and I saw what a stupid girl I was, and felt so ashamed. I picked up one stick, and started to rub it hard against another, but I knew in a minute that it was not going to work, and it made my hands sore. My soft, pathetic hands. I hated them then, and I rubbed the sticks together, still harder, in a kind of rage, until my fingers bled and I crouched over the dead ashes, crying bitter tears into the mess.

But, of course, tears helped nothing. The wind howled through the trees in spite of them. The rain came down still, in tiny drops, like a relentless mist falling. And after I had finished crying I sat up a little and drew my shawl about me, and thought of Cavendish Square, of dinner being served, the fires burning in the grates, the soft dry bed in my old room. And I realized that, cold and defeated as I was, I hankered after none of these things, but only after my Valentin, my darling: I longed only for his return. And I swore to myself that I would watch, with care, when next he lit the fire. I would watch, and learn everything, and make him a good Romani wife.

I fell fast asleep, propped against the steps, and when I woke again it was so dark I could not see my hand in front of my face. For a moment I thought my eyes were trapped shut, but when I looked up into the sky I could see a thin crescent moon, as mean as my dinner had been, like a bare bone through the cloud. No stars, as there had been the night before: as if they had gone away with my love.

I had not seen before how very black the night is in the countryside, when Valentin had been there, to light a torch and hold me to him. In London it is never so dark. There are always lights burning somewhere – yet there, in that field, as I looked around me into the thick night I saw not one lonely spark, and I grew very afraid, and felt my way up the steps to the door of the wagon, and pulled it open. Of course it was no lighter inside than out: there were no servants to light the lamps, only the same black tar darkness, like the bottom of a pit. I stood on the threshold, wondering what creeping things were there to keep me company, and then I felt my way over to the little bed at the back, and climbed under the coverlet. My ears seemed to strain against the sides of my head, twitching with every tiny sound: the footsteps of a fruit fly, a lonely cricket, the grass growing outside. And then another sound that I could not make out at first: just a part of the background of sounds, like the river flowing behind the hill. But growing slowly louder, and separating from the landscape, bit by bit, until I could hear rustling and the thud of a horse's hoofs, and the murmur of voices. Low voices, muttering, coming across the field towards me. Something stopped me jumping up and looking out to see who was there. I bent my very nerves towards the sound, tight as piano wire, but I heard no more of them, till the snort of a horse's breath, sudden, on the other side of the window, which made me start, and the jangle of a bridle as it shook its head.

And then a gruff voice spoke: 'Cold as death,' it said.

A female voice answered: 'Has she gone?'

And then the gruff voice again: 'I don't like it.'

'Open the door,' said she.

And with that the door opened, cautiously, and a lamp came around it, and then a face, and as I was about to scream with terror I heard a shout: 'She is here!' And a hushing, and I recognized the face of my beloved – and behind him, my dearest friend, Emily.

I expect I startled them, leaping from the bed. For a moment they looked at me as if I was a stranger, and their eyes in the torchlight were blank and dark – but they recovered themselves, and were all smiles then.

'Heavens! But you gave us a funny turn, my dear Tabitha,' said Emily, and we laughed at that. 'We thought you had been taken! The fire was cold, and the light was out, and we feared you were lost to us.'

Valentin was quiet for a minute or two, and when he spoke he was angry. His voice shook, and his hands a little, too, though he brought them under control. I knew I had given him a fright, and I felt more foolish than ever before.

'Why was the fire cold?' he demanded. 'And the lamp. What stupidity is this?'

'Hush yourself,' said Emily. 'Don't be harsh. Poor Tabitha has been frightened, I expect.' She took my scratched hands in hers. 'What was she supposed to do for herself here, on her own? She is a lady. And quite unaccustomed to the ways of travelling folk.'

'But I can learn!' I told them. 'I do not wish to be a lady, or to be back at Cavendish Square. If only you will teach me these things, I will learn.'

Valentin looked at me a while, with his eyes glittering in the darkness, and he frightened me, but my belly stirred with the fire I had felt before, watching his manful hands upon the horse's reins.

'Yes, you will,' he said.

Once I had recovered myself from the shock of their arrival, and the delight of seeing my dear Emily and come to my senses again, my first thought was that, as joyous as it was to see her, perhaps it meant something was awry. Perhaps my father had not believed her story, or the search was drawing near. I had opened my mouth to ask her, 'What of my mother? Is she very distressed? Is there trouble coming?' but I closed it again. Of course my poor mother was distressed. Most likely she was tearing the hair from her head; most likely I had killed her with the shock of my disappearing, the shame and disgrace upon my family. I did not want to know. I decided that if Emily had bad news to tell me she would do it in her own good time.

But she did not. No ill tidings came. And I was so pleased at that I quite forgot the question of what she had come for.

*

I heard Valentin and Emily quarrelling many times that week. Or rather, mostly, I saw it. They would set off across the field to the stream to fetch water, or to the village for bread, or the farm for eggs ('A girl cannot live by hedgehog alone,' said Emily!) – together, always together, so that the country folk would think they were a married pair, starting out, perhaps, to make their own way, and not that Valentin was a lone gypsy man, of whom they would have been suspicious – and on their way back I would see them where they had stopped at the bottom of the field, so as to spare me hearing them: Emily leaning forward, wagging a finger at him, he slapping his forehead, clenching his fists. I knew they were quarrelling about me. They had told me about the newspaper reports, and the handbills asking for information of my whereabouts, for witnesses to come forward. I knew that Emily thought that Valentin should have left me where I was, that it was a foolish venture and that I would have been better in my old life, and I knew she felt bad for her part in bringing me to him only to be as good as his servant, for I was not his wife still. All this she told me later, and when I promised her that I was happy, though the life could be hard and comfortless perhaps, and Valentin a little harsh (as Emily had told me the Romani men are), she would not talk of it, but only turned her head away and gazed into the fire. And it was the next day, as I saw them at the bottom of the field, facing each other again, stabbing at the air with pointed fingers – and felt, again, in my stupid way, the pang of jealousy at seeing them together – it was then that I thought, or rather, felt, that Emily was in love with Valentin herself.

I was obliged to sit down suddenly at this revelation, for it was such a shock, and yet so crystal clear. I thought back along the path of our acquaintance and tried to pinpoint when it was that it might have begun. Had she secretly wanted him back in London, when he and I first met? No, for she would never have helped me to escape. It was the day she left us, I decided. I remembered them up on the horse's back together: how they had looked such a handsome couple, how I had hoped he would not notice the mysterious charm that had come upon her suddenly; how it had stung me to watch them ride away and the relief I had felt when he returned without her. She had fallen in love with him that very day! She must have sat on the train for London, looking out of the window at the rolling fields and dreaming of him, longing, wanting him for herself. Why else would she have come back? The more I thought of it, the more the pieces seemed to fall into a picture. Poor Emily, I thought, she cannot help herself. No woman could have resisted Valentin once she saw him on the road, driving that horse, with his strong hands and his dark gypsy eyes, for he looked like the king of Egypt himself. And though I could not quite look at Emily when she came back up the hill, and though I think she noticed that I was quiet at her chatter, how could I blame her for falling in love with him?

But all the same I began to wonder when she was to leave, and to wish it would be soon.

I started to watch her with Valentin, the little glances she stole, the frigid demeanour she took on when she spoke to him, when underneath it I could see her beating heart. I thought to ask him why she was with us still, and when she might go, but in truth I was afraid to. Perhaps, even then, I was afraid of what the answer would be. Besides it is not for the gypsy women to know the men's business. That was the response to all my questions – when would I meet his family? Why had we gone on apart from them? What was it that he had to attend to back towards London, and what of the scratches he had returned with? Deep, sore scratches on his back: who had done this thing to him, and how? Every time he gave the same reply: 'Go about your own business, woman! And do not vex me with questions.' I felt that the next time it was given it would be served with a slap.

You may think Valentin a gruff, cruel man. Truly he was not. He was sweet, and gentle too, only it was his way. And if he was a tyrant, it made no difference to me. I loved him more every day, with a passion that alarmed me sometimes. I seemed to be changing inside myself: I was tougher, stronger. I could build fires and cook stew. I washed clothes in a bowl by the fire, and gathered nettles and swept the camp clean. And I could not have been more attached to Valentin, and less able to leave him, than if he had chained me to the wheels of that painted wagon.

It was but a week that Emily was with us, but such a long one, and it was so very quickly that I began to resent her. As I watched them go down the field together I would seethe with a jealous fury, like a slow-smouldering coal burning a hole in my stomach, though I knew I could not be seen in the village. And when they returned even then she never left us alone, not for one minute, and I began to starve for want of his kisses and his love. What she had done for me, she seemed to want undone.

And it was more as an enemy I began to see her then than as a friend.

Chapter Eight

Rose

I am singing a little song when the warden next looks in on me: at the window, as I watch the men sweeping the litter from the street. She is scowling at my back – I can hear it in the tone of her voice.

'You have another visitor,' she says, sour as lemons. She is jealous, I expect, at my burgeoning social calendar, so much busier than her own. It is her own fault, after all, for having such a job and such a hairy mole upon her face.

'Do see them in,' I tell her airily, over my shoulder. The sight of her gargoyle visage will put me off my dinner.

'Good evening, Rose,' says a familiar voice. I spin round. It is Lady Quayle, stepping into my cell, looking rather nervously about her, trying not to brush her skirts against the filthy walls.

'Why, Lady Quayle!' I exclaim, 'Whatever are you doing in this place?' She looks at me then with haunted eyes, a little vacant, as if she were sleepwalking.

'Oh, Rose,' she says. 'Such a dreadful thing!'

I am about to tell her everything, protest my innocence,

explain how I came to be at that junction on the Kent Road at Deptford. But as I look at her I can tell there is no need. Her skin is pale, her hands shake. Her gaze is wide, searching my face as if all the answers might be there.

'What is it, my lady?'

She opens her reticule, and takes from it a small purse, which she unties to reveal a bundle of white handkerchief, wrapped around many times. She shudders, draws her own lace hanky across her face. Even before I see the bloodstains upon the cloth parcel I know what is inside.

'Oh, Rose,' she whispers. 'Such a ghastly thing! But only look, I beg of you, and tell me for certain.'

She puts this small bundle into my hands. Even as she does she seems to be relieved of a great terrible burden, and I seem to shoulder one, though it weighs no more than a dead mouse. She raises her eyes to mine, and they are red with weeping, but blank also, a little mad with horror.

'I do not believe . . .' she says, '. . . I do not believe that this is Tabitha's finger.'

Lord Quayle would not let her see it at first, for he thought it too ghastly a sight for feminine eyes – but, then, what terrors could a mere finger hold for a mother who has already suffered the abduction of their daughter and the fear of what might happen to her? as Lady Quayle so eloquently puts it. As soon as she had laid eyes on it she had known it did not belong on her daughter's hand, but her husband had dismissed her – what nonsense! How was she to identify her daughter from a single finger! He had never heard such tosh in all his life! So she stole it from under the nose of the butler, who had been charged with keeping it on ice, along with the ransom demand it came with, which she found in Lord Quayle's desk.

The note smells of tobacco, and wickedness, and this is what it says:

Lord Quayle

Here is one of your daughter's pretty digits, just as we promised you. We hope it will make you see sense. Do not fail us again or more will follow. Bring the money and come alone this time – to the same spot, Friday week, at nine o'clock. And this time leave your friends at home. Do not play games with us, good sir. Have a care for your dear Tabitha, sat here in the dark with her nine fingers.

See it done right this time.

It is a Mercury finger – that is, a little finger; hewn off with one blow, I would say – or taken off, perhaps, in the jamb of a heavy door. It is small and slim, with a tapered fingertip, and Lady Quayle is quite right. It is not Tabitha's finger. Tabitha has blunt, strong hands, and this finger comes from someone with closed, cautious paws.

Like those of a little mouse.

This finger belongs to Emily.

*

This new ransom demand, with its unhappy accompaniment, throws Lord Quayle and the police into confusion, my lady tells me. Does this then mean that I am innocent, or that my accomplices are acting without me? What then, do I know, and how far can it be trusted? And her assertion that it is not Miss Tabitha Quayle's finger has been brushed aside – for if it is not hers, then whose is it? And are they then to assume that her captors are not men of their word or, indeed, that they are no longer holding her? And if so, where has she gone? Confounded, Lord Quayle and the police have decided to comply with the demands of the letter. At least that is what they have told Lady Quayle, and she believes them. Setting another trap for these ruthless men would be a foolish thing to do – seeing as poor Tabitha, as far as they are concerned, has already lost a finger. She is certain they will not risk it.

I tell her I am sure she is right, that they will not put poor Tabitha at risk.

I do not tell her who the severed digit belongs to. It would be altogether too confusing for her. I am confused enough myself – too much to explain such a turn-up. And it would be quite beyond poor Lady Quayle's comprehension to find that her own dear daughter has any part in such an evil deed.

So I keep it to myself, and I am left with an unhappy feeling that I have failed Emily – though she was certainly not a good girl (for who am I to judge her?) and though I don't suppose there is anything I might have done. It was there, her fortune, marked on the palm of her hand, as plain as black and white.

Beware the fatal influence of a woman.

And now it is too late.

*

I am released the next day. Plainly I have not been involved in the severing of this poor finger, and Lady Quayle herself testifies to my good character. I may be a gypsy, she tells them, but she has found me to be trustworthy in all our dealings, and she believes I have had no part at all in the sorry affair. The question of why she did not speak up to this effect a week ago – or, indeed, at my trial – goes unanswered.

*

Emily comes to me that night in a dream, as I sleep in my soft bed upstairs at the Buttered Bun. She stretches her hands out in front of her: I see the ugly stump of her severed finger, her accusing hollow eyes. *Only you know*, she says. *Only you.*

I wake in the dark with a start.

Only I know who has finished poor Miss Emily. A golden-haired assassin, with hard blue eyes, like wet stones, and murder written on the palm of her right hand. The palm, you see, never lies.

I lie and look at the ceiling. I hear a horse's hoofs upon the cobbles outside and a lonely cock crow in the distance over towards Seven Dials, and I wonder if it was Tabitha herself, or her philanderer who cut the dead digit from that hand: the one he held at the Argyll Rooms, under the table, while his golden-haired lady watched the dance-floor swirl below. And I wonder what has happened out there among the ripening fields to turn all their fortunes about so, and to turn Miss Tabitha from prisoner to accomplice.

*

'Well thank goodness it's done with,' says Lillie, over *à la mode Beef*, toasting me with a glass of sham. 'I thought you might've come a proper cropper there, I don't mind telling you now. It gave me an awful turn.'

'Well, my dear,' I tell her, 'I was worried myself. You did me proud, Miss Lillie. Eternal thanks.' We chink glasses and drink. 'This is a very good dinner,' I remark. 'How's business going on?'

'Well,' says Lillie, 'funny you should ask. What with worrying about you, and with poor Lady Quayle's daughter missing – well, I'd let her alone for a while, it didn't seem the right thing to do. Vulgar, let's say. And that brown worsted dress is so itchy. So things were getting a little on the tight side. Anyhow, yesterday afternoon she called for me and gave me twenty pounds from her husband's desk! To spread among the unfortunate girls of St Giles! So I told her thank you very much. And here it is.' She passes me a cut under the table and we order more drinks.

*

Lady Quayle sends me a message by surly footman the very next week. I expect she has suffered pangs of guilty conscience at leaving me to rot in jail for eight days. The message mentions nothing of it, but I am to come to the front door this evening, where I am welcomed by my friend the footman, who does not look directly at me, but only past my left ear. As I am shown in upstairs, Lady Quayle greets me with a glass of fizz – of all the things in the world I might expect to be waiting for me at the top of the Quayle staircase!

'A toast to your liberty, Rose,' she says. And really it is very kind of her. She is not obliged to care about my liberty at all. And I must say I do not blame her for having been suspicious about me, about my motives, or my character, for she really doesn't know me from Adam. We drink to it, anyway, liberty, and love, and good fortune. The sham is very good indeed, but perhaps not cold enough. Good fortune brings her neatly to the next point.

'You told me, my dear,' she says, with a rueful sigh. 'No one can say you did not warn me.'

'Warn you, my lady?'

'You told me what would happen, and I dismissed it. "Do not let Tabitha go away with Emily," you said. Indeed, you urged me to prevent it.' Lady Quayle has drained her glass and I fear that she may already be a bit tipsy.

'You told me, my dear, and I did not listen, I did not listen at all, and now look where we are! My daughter is gone, and who knows where? And though we are to pay the ransom – which Lord Quayle was so happy to return with the last time one might have thought he had chosen it to bring home over his own dear daughter – though we are to pay it over this Friday instead, with each day that passes the fear that I may never see her again grows a little stronger for I have the strangest feeling . . .' She frowns at the wallpaper, as if trying to catch a lost thought.

'What is it, my lady?' She stares through the spot, a little fuzzy from the sham.

'I cannot help but think,' she says, 'that perhaps Tabitha is not taken at all, but rather gone of her own volition. There is something not right in all of this. If it is not her . . . finger in that ghastly package, then why has she not returned home? The only sense I can make of it is that either she has perished, or that she does not want to return. And a little voice in my head tells me that she is not dead, no, there is something too . . . *robust* about Tabitha for that to be so.'

Now Lady Quayle is stabbing in the dark, but razor sharp. She astounds me. I hope she does not turn these shiny new wits upon the question of Miss Lillie Daley and her brown worsted dress.

She turns her glassy eyes to mine, swimming in sham and confusion. 'How, Rose, how could that be true? What could I have done to deserve such an injury? I pray that it is not so!'

Lady Quayle does not make it altogether clear whether she would be happier for Tabitha to be dead, or for parts of her to be hewn off and posted through the letterbox. Better, surely, for her to have run away. But I do not trouble her with this thought.

And just as I am coughing up something comforting to say, and wondering why she has brought me here today, she thrusts out her hand, palm up. 'Tell me,' she says, slurring just a little. 'Tell me, Rose . . .' She tails off, and sits, looking, disconsolate, at her hand.

'You must cross my palm with silver first, my lady,' I say.

Lady Quayle has been fretting very much of late: her palms are striped with tiny worry lines. I have not looked at them for some time and, as if to keep me up with the news, all the events of the past few weeks are recorded here, like newspaper clippings. First I see the Fate line, which was so weak as to be invisible before. It begins with Lillie, of course, halfway up my lady's palm, marking the very moment, on the steps of the Haymarket theatre, that her new sense of purpose was born; I see Lady Quayle's flushed face there, glowing in the foyer lights as she resolves to save the red rosette girl's wretched soul, and I feel a little wretched myself, as I think of the deceit her noble sentiments stand upon. I see our own first meeting, marked upon the Head line, with a tiny slash. I see poor Lady Quayle's lonely heart, her distracted husband. A deep worry line across the Mount of Venus that joins the Vital on the day Emily came back alone, and another next to it – marking the parcel post, no doubt. And then a tiny break in her Heart line: the empty space that Tabitha has left. I look up at her sad, clouded face. Something like remorse, or sympathy, stirs in my chest: perhaps the sham is making me giddy too.

'Do you see her coming home, Rose?' she says. Her voice is a hazy croak, like a broken clock chiming. I look back down again, for good omens, luck, a happy outcome, and if there are none I shall lie to her, for I can't bear to see her heart break. I pull her hand closer to the lamp, take out my optical glass, and turn all the wishes of my dishonest heart towards my lady's cause. And there – there it is! A tiny star, under the Jupiter finger, the sign of hope, and wishes fulfilled – the brightest thing I have seen since the sun shining through the open gates of Horsemonger Lane.

'Yes, my lady!' I cry. 'She will come home. Before the summer is out!'

There is one person not mentioned in all of this. My lady seems to have quite forgotten her. She is not referred to, or asked after – I do not believe, indeed, that Lady Quayle has noticed she is gone. Poor Emily. She was only a shopgirl, after all. She is absent even from my lady's palm. It is as if she had never existed at all.

*

Lady Quayle is much cheered by the news. So much so, indeed, that she calls me back to hear it again the very next morning. The ransom is due tomorrow. I am asked to elaborate a little: will Tabitha come back alive? A good enough question! Yes, she will come back alive. And in good health, with all her parts intact? Safe to say, with all her parts intact – except one perhaps, a private one I do not mention. Alone? I can't be sure. And how? I tell her that, difficult as it may be, she must not fret, but trust instead in Providence and the protection of the good Lord. God, that is, and not Lord Quayle. Who, incidentally, she says she has not seen for a week. She breathes a satisfied sigh and drops her shoulders a little.

'Now tell me, Rose,' she says, stretching her hand across the table again, 'what of Annie Atkins?'

For a moment I cannot place Annie Atkins. Her name rings a loud bell in my head but I struggle to put a face to it: so many fretful things have fallen on my lady's plate since we last spoke of her that I am surprised to hear her mention the poor girl at all. And, like Lillie, I had thought to let the whole business go, for a while anyhow. It is somewhat of a vulgar concern with things the way they are. And that brown worsted dress is so very itchy.

But now that Lady Quayle is *asking* after Annie Atkins, I might be persuaded to take it up again – though I haven't the heart for the crystal ball. Instead I show her the proud new Fate line that runs up the centre of her palm. It may be faint but it is straight, indeed.

'Oh!' she says. 'Was it not there before?'

'It was not my lady.'

'Well,' she says, 'it is true that I do feel my life to have a new purpose, and I am thoroughly pleased with it. Although I must confess I have neglected the duties of my calling some-what, lately.'

'No one could blame you for that, my lady,' I tell her.

'Perhaps not. But all the same, I shall look her up this afternoon, I think.' She gives a little sigh of satisfaction at the morning's revelations. 'Thank you, Rose, my dear. Do you think you might bring the crystal ball the next time you visit?'

*

Needless to say, I do not revisit that crossroads on the Kent road, by Deptford, the second time the ransom is to be delivered. But I hear from Lady Quayle that all their efforts were in vain. No one came to collect it, she tells me: the police waited in the dark until midnight and repaired to their station frustrated men. The only signs of life, apparently, were a man on horseback, with a woman pulled up behind him, wrapped in layers of clothing, scarves around their dark heads; the police let them pass undisturbed. Gypsies! Why did they not think to stop them? Well, says Lady Quayle, had not Emily painted a vivid picture of heavy-set, bearded men who took Tabitha?

And could these two have been further from that description? Besides, everyone knows that, dishonest as the gypsies are . . . here she stops, flushes awkwardly and begs my pardon: she did not mean any offence by it, nor, indeed, did she mean to refer to me, but mustn't I have heard of the reputation that goes before the gypsy folk? – not, of course, that she subscribes to that view (I let her away with it) . . . Dishonest as they are perceived to be, the travelling gypsy people keep to themselves. Furthermore, they do not read or write – ransom notes or anything else. And so, you see, they could have had nothing to do with it at all.

And now how I wish I had been at that crossroads! I would have run down that horse, seized the man and flung back the hood of his lady's cloak with my own bare hands – for if it was not Miss Tabitha Quayle underneath it I will skin my own palms and burn my grandmother's cards and I will never read another fortune again. Who else could it be but she?

Only for want of proof does the Queen's Counsel spare me the gallows. And now, with no one besides in the frame, I feel those dark accusations clouding the sky above me, coming back to hang over my head.

*Report made this 4th August 1860 by Sgt Robert Duff
of the Great Marlborough St police office*

This afternoon I have conducted a short interview with Miss
Rose Lee, who was released from Horsemonger Lane gaol
Monday last. The questioning took place at the Buttered Bun
coffee shop, Soho Square, in a back room as directed by the
proprietress, one Mrs Bunion, a most irksome woman, who
told us quite freely that she 'held no truck with peelers'. At
any rate, I was able to ask Miss Lee what she made of Lady
Quayle's extraordinary claim that the severed digit received at
27 Cavendish Square last week does not belong to her daughter
Tabitha. She said she saw nothing extraordinary about it.
Indeed, she said, Lady Quayle was Tabitha's 'own dear mother'
and was bound to know these things, which may be supposed
to be true enough, although Lady Quayle has been distressed
these last few weeks and may be lacking in her usual faculty
of objective judgement.

When I put this to Miss Lee she revealed that Lady Quayle
had been to see her at Horsemonger Lane and shown her said
digit. And, having seen it with her own eyes, she could not
only confirm that it did not belong to Miss Tabitha Quayle
but could reveal the identity of its rightful owner. In her
opinion, it was cut from the hand of Miss Emily Budd: the
young lady who accompanied Miss Tabitha on her journey to
St Leonard's. She could confirm this supposition, she said,
because she had read Miss Budd's palm on two occasions, and
recognized it. Hands and, indeed, fingers, she said, were as

distinct to her as faces. And where did she suppose Miss Emily Budd was now?

'Dead in a ditch,' she said, in a most impertinent tone. And what of Miss Tabitha? I asked her then. 'Out on the open road,' she replied. With whom? 'Who knows?' she said. So, then, I asked her, were we to suppose that Miss Tabitha might be responsible in some way for Miss Budd's disappearance? 'You may suppose what you like,' she told me. I put it to her, did she not think it unlikely that a lady from such a privileged background would give up the comforts of her grand home to travel the byways of the land in a dusty cart with this person, or persons, unknown? 'The Roma do not drive carts,' said she, 'but wagons, and they keep them spotless clean.' And, she added, perhaps Miss Tabitha had been bored with her comfortable life and wanted for excitement. Perhaps, she said, she had 'given up everything for love'.

At that point I brought the questioning to a close, seeing that we were wasting time. It is well known that the gypsy people have a disregard for the law and the work of the police and I fear the witness is being deliberately backward. Furthermore, in my opinion, Miss Rose Lee will say anything to divert suspicion from herself. It is my belief that she was involved in the abduction of Lady Tabitha Quayle and, furthermore, that she alerted her accomplices to the risk of capture at the drop-off point. I propose to put her under surveillance until some firm evidence of her guilt is found.

Chapter Nine

Tabitha

All at once, a week to the day that she had arrived, Emily was gone. They rose with the lark and set off one morning, she and Valentin, and were away an hour or more. I began to worry – what could have happened to them? Had they been found out? Was a search party coming for me? A policeman? Or – this the worst of idea of all – had she charmed him somehow, spirited him away, as I had known she would? For I had seen it in her eyes every day. How had I let her steal him from me? I paced the camp, back and forth, back and forth, in agitation at this thought. And how long must I wait? I wanted to go and search for him but I knew I must not.

And then I saw him, coming up the hill. I wanted to shout. I looked for her to appear round the hedgerow behind him.

He came up to the edge of the camp and stopped, the sun shining on his back, lighting a halo around him. I could not see his face against the glare of it. We stood for a moment.

'Emily is gone,' he said.

Only that. Emily is gone.

He tore his shirt off and threw it on the ground. When I

washed it later I saw blood upon it. Splashes of blood, like ink blots. Like the splashes of blood when you cut the head off a rabbit.

*

We left not an hour later, headed south-west with the sun climbing the sky behind us. It seemed to point hot fingers after us, shine a light on our dark hearts. We didn't say a word. The only sounds were the hoofs of the poor horse, labouring in the heat as if to atone for our sin, and the birds jeering from the trees. Did I care? I did not. I sat at the front of the wagon next to my love and I looked at the road ahead and I knew I had crossed some bridge that was burning at my back. I was happy for it. Let us be going down the road to hell! I thought. Let us leave the world of houses and shops, ladies, chatter, and dinners and society behind! I couldn't give tuppence for any of it. And I shall never go back.

A man watched us from behind his garden gate as we went by. I smiled but he did not smile back. At the end of the lane a woman hurried her children away.

We stopped by a wood, as remote a spot as we could find, next to a little stream. The sun was beginning to climb down the sky. I gathered wood while Valentin caught something for dinner: he went out for trout but came back with a hedgehog as I was starting the fire. He killed it with a blow to the head – so skilfully, so quickly, it could not have hurt the poor crea-ture – and, standing on the front legs, he pulled it tight and shaved off the bristles. I thought of the blood spots on his shirt again, and I wanted to ask him about Emily, but I dared not.

He was blackening the hotchi over the fire by the time I plucked up the courage to ask.

'Where did Emily go?' I said, trying to make the question sound as if it were an incidental thought that had just popped into my head.

He looked at me then, quite hard, and said, 'Emily who?' He took his knife and opened the hotchi along the back to gut it. I knew he had to concentrate for this part and I must not ask him silly questions. I was curious – but not so much that I mentioned it again. It was better not to know what had happened, I thought to myself.

We ate as the dark came down. He did not look at me but stared into the fire, throwing the bones into it as he picked them clean. At last, just as I thought he would never look at me or talk to me again, he spoke. 'Do you love me, Tabitha?' he said.

'Yes, I do,' I declared. 'With all my heart and every breath in my body.'

He laughed then, softly, and put out his hand to stroke my cheek. He slid it down to my shoulder and then my waist, and he gripped me there with a big, firm hand, and squeezed me slowly.

'That's good,' he murmured, as he pulled me to him, grazing my face with the bristles on his chin. 'Good girl.'

*

We spent four blissful days by that stream, walking the hedge-rows, sleeping in the dappled sun, looking into the fire at night, at the dancing shapes, dragons and devils. He said we would join his family in Kent, come August. Would they not miss him? Not until September, when the hopping starts, he said. Did he not miss them? I asked him, but he said, no, he was happy. He wanted to keep me to himself, just a while longer.

I would have liked to meet them, travel with them, roam the roads, free and far away. I never have picked fruit, or hops: I should have liked to try my hand at it. But now, after all that has passed between, it may never happen.

*

When we awoke the next morning there were men at the top of the field. Two men, with a dog. 'Wait here,' he told me, and went up to speak to them. I watched him at the top of the field, from inside the wagon, as he had said. When he came back he said we must leave. He cursed and spat at the ground. 'Whatever is wrong?' I asked him.

'It is a Friday,' he said. 'It is bad luck to move on a Friday.'

I threw my arms around his neck. 'Never mind, my love,' I told him. 'I will bring you luck!' Silly girl. It seems such a very stupid thing to say now.

Anyhow, we packed up our things and raked over the fire and made to go. And just as I was stowing the pots and pans away a dreadful thing happened: the very worst omen of all. Do you know what it is? A bird flew into the wagon – straight in through the door – a little bird, a finch, or something like it. It bumped into the looking glass that hung above the larder and went into a frenzy, flapping its wings about and hurling itself at the walls. I expect it was very frightened. I chased it around the wagon but I could not catch it and I only seemed to make it more frantic: I thought it would beat itself to death or break its tiny neck, crashing into the glass, with a ghastly shrieking and feathers beating – and then, as suddenly as it had come in, it found the door again and was gone.

I swept up the little feathers it had left behind. Valentin had been at the water with the horse and he had not seen it. I didn't tell him it had been there.

*

We moved on, some ten miles or so down the road, and camped again. Valentin seemed wary: he looked all about him as he parked the wagon and watered the horse. He went out for hours, and came back with a hare. As we ate that evening he was sullen and quiet. Only after I had washed the dishes and put everything away for the night did he catch my hand and pull me down on to his lap. We slept that night and the next in each other's arms, with only the calling of the night birds and the whistle of the wind outside for company.

*

I woke alone on the third night. Valentin was not by the fire, the horse was gone. A great full moon lit the meadow, not a breath of wind stirred the trees: they stood still and ghostly, watching me as I sat upon the painted steps, wrapped in the blanket, looking out over the silver fields. A fox came out of the hedgerow and stopped to look at me, one paw held from

132

the ground, his wild tail a frozen banner. And then, with a flick of it, he was gone, as if I had dreamed him.

When I fell asleep on the step I was visited by the strangest things. I could see the meadow, and the trees, and everything about me, just the same as if I had been awake. Only now a wind started to blow in the bushes at the bottom of the meadow, and it travelled up toward the wagon where I sat, and as it came it gathered itself into a ball, and when it reached the bottom of the wagon steps it dropped Valentin before me, on to his feet, and he stood there with the blowing wind turning circles about him, pulling at his shirt and his dark Romani hair and then, very suddenly, it was still, and deathly quiet; and he started up the steps towards me. I was afraid, but riveted to the spot. And then I felt his breath on my neck and heard a whispering in my ear, like the sound of dead leaves rustling.

I shall keep you, I thought it said. *To the end of the road.*

And with that, it seemed, I woke, and there he was, lifting me from the step, like a bundle of rags, in his arms, and without a word he took me into the wagon. He dropped me on the bed and tore open his belt and thrust into me, slow and hard, looking at my face in the silvery half-light from the window, as if he had never seen me before.

When morning came, we had packed up and gone.

Chapter Ten

Rose

I do not like Oxford Street. It is altogether too long. But this fine morning sees me venture down it to visit Emily's shop. The sunshine is at odds with the dark clouds gathering in my head, the sensation of that knotted rope against my throat; my collar feels too tight around my neck. When I looked out over Soho Square this morning the first thing I saw was a policeman watching the Buttered Bun. Perhaps he was merely resting on the corner, or being tempted by the frying bacon, but it seemed to me he stood rather too long on that spot, across from my window.

I do not know what I hope to gain from calling at the shop. But I mean to find poor Emily's fancy man, somehow, and I do not know where else to start. If the shop is open at all I might find something to set me in the right direction, anything – perhaps discover his name, or her mother's address.

At least I will come away with new buttons for my summer overcoat, which will be something, even if I shall be sewing them on to a condemned woman's clothes.

I am so lost in my own thoughts that I almost walk past the little shop. It is something in the window that catches my eye. That little tray of wooden flowers, that I saw before: Romani men carve them from elder, when they are weary of making pegs. Pretty things they are too: pretty things for pretty women. And now I look up, and see that this is the place. A sign on the back of the door announces that it is open. And so I go in. A bell rings as I step across the mat, and I almost expect Emily to look up from behind the counter. But, of course, she does not. Instead it is another mousy creature, with neat white hands and pearly teeth.

'Good morning,' she says.

'Good morning to you, miss,' I reply. 'I am after light coat buttons.'

Well, she pulls out a drawer of them, and as I am looking through it, I am working my way round to asking after poor dead Miss Emily Mouse. At last I say, 'There was a girl here before, some two or three weeks gone now, not unlike yourself my dear.' I pause nonchalantly, considering the blue shell button in my hand.

'You must be thinking of Emily,' she says.

'Yes, Emily.' I pick out a small horn button and lay it on the counter next to the blue one.

'Poor dear Emily,' says she.

'Poor dear Emily indeed.' I sigh, laying down another button in the row and looking up to meet her innocent gaze. 'So, you have heard the news.'

'Why, yes, to my great regret, of course,' says she. 'That is the reason I am here at all. She managed the shop perfectly well by herself, you know, before. She never needed so much as a day off, or a hand to help her.'

'Quite so. What a bitter twist of Fate it is.' I bow my head and lower my solemn eyes.

'It is a terrible business,' says the pearly-toothed girl. 'I shudder to imagine it.' Duly she obliges with a modest shudder. Having illustrated her feelings so, she turns her interest to me. 'I expect you are a friend of the family?' she enquires.

You can expect whatever you like, cheeky miss, I want to tell her. But instead I say: 'I am a distant cousin on her mother's side. We had made our acquaintance only very recently.'

'Well,' she says, 'it must have been such a shock for her family. I expect you all must be a great comfort to one another.'

All this expecting and commiserating is very personable but it is getting me nowhere. I move across to the window, and look at the tray of Romani flowers, putting my head a little to the side as if my eye had fallen on them by chance. 'These are uncommonly charming,' I say. 'Wherever do they come from?'

She looks over to see what I may be referring to. 'Oh,' she says, 'are they not the quaintest thing! I believe a Romani gypsy man brings them. I have seen him about here before. He is a handsome fellow if ever you saw one!' She blushes sweetly at the memory of him, even though just a moment before she was bemoaning the loss of her dead friend.

I pick out a dandelion. It is my favourite flower. Hardy and bright, and yellow as egg yolk. She has turned away to wrap it when the bell rings behind us with the door opening. As someone steps over the mat there is a crash and a cry, and the sound of coins scattering across the floor. We turn to see a small woman crouched over the mess, trying to pick up her strewn belongings with one hand – for the other is in a sling.

'Why, Miss Emily!' says the shopgirl. 'Are you quite all right?'

My ears seem to contract at the sound of that name. The crouched figure looks up from the floor, her face coming out like a ghost's from behind the brim of her hat. It is a small face, with wide grey eyes, sharp, like a little mouse.

It is she. Plain as day.

I must do better at hiding my shock than I imagine. I feel that my face blanches as white as clean bones and my eyes bulge from their sockets. But Miss Emily only says, 'Oh! Good morning, Miss Rose. I must have startled you. What a surprise to see you in my little shop.'

And I only reply, 'Well, Miss Emily, I have come for buttons,' and then, 'Let me help you with these things.' And I stoop to gather up her scattered effects. As I pick up coins, and papers, and pins, my mind is a-whirl with question marks, and tumbling pieces of a picture that do not fit. A poor dead Emily laid out, as I have imagined her, beneath a hedgerow in some lonely lane. Her carefree blue-eyed killer laughing and shaking her golden ringlets at the winding road. That little square palm, the dark spot upon it; that butchered finger, and the Romani couple riding by the drop-off spot; and Emily Budd, now, here on her own with her bandaged hand. And quite another picture starts to come together. There are many ways one might account for all of these things. But at the centre of it is a dreadful vision of Miss Emily Mouse holding her own hand out for someone to hack off her finger.

Or – taking it off herself.

The thought makes me feel quite sick, and faint, and a little frightened. I retrieve the last coin, which has rolled under a small table of ribbons, and return it to her, looking into her grey eyes, which seem to belong to quite another person looking out through Miss Emily Mouse's little face.

'Thank you,' she says. 'I am so clumsy with this one arm. Charlotte has told me not to carry anything.'

'Whatever has happened?' I ask her.

'Would you believe?' she says. 'I was set upon in the park last week by two villainous men' – I gasp, duly horrified, though more at Miss Emily Mouse's front than at her story – 'and was thrown to the ground in the ensuing struggle. Although I am happy to say that they made off without the takings, all the bones in my hand are fractured, and will take several weeks to heal, the doctor tells me. It is quite black – and most unsightly – and so, you see, I have covered it up, over the bandage.' Barefaced as a new-born baby she tells me this, and then smiles, a little wounded but bearing it bravely. Without so much as the quiver of an eyelash.

The hand is a shapeless bundle, sticking stiffly out from the sling around her neck, the ends of her fingers hidden. No one would ever tell that one was missing.

Well, I come out of there with my head swimming, but a spring in my step and hope, as well as buttons. I must see Lady Quayle. I must reveal Emily's secret. I repair to the Buttered Bun to think.

*

138

'He's been there all morning, like a great stuffed monkey,' says Mrs Bunion. 'I've a mind to go and poke him in the eye.' The policeman across the road spots us peering through the window at him and colours a little under his imposing hat, which looks a size too large. He seems awkward: he shuffles his feet, and looks away, as if he had just spotted something of interest in the treetops around the square – a rare bird, perhaps – and was not really watching the Buttered Bun at all. Any other day I might have laughed at him. But I seem to hear Holy Trinity's bells ringing those twelve dread chimes in my head – and he, twitching on the corner in his big hat, looks like the harbinger of doom.

'I don't have no truck with peelers,' says Mrs Bunion, for the third time this morning.

'No, Mrs B.'

'I'll go out there and knock his hat off if he hasn't gone by twelve.'

'I think we should just let him alone, Mrs B.'

She looks him up and down, chewing it over. 'Very well, dear,' she says at last. 'But I won't serve him if he comes in. I'll knock him flat.'

'Good enough,' I tell her.

She turns to me, eyes dark black like currants. 'It's not like you, dear, to draw attention to yourself,' she says. 'I thought you was in the clear.'

'Well, I know, Mrs B. So did I.'

*

Lady Quayle is fairly busting her stays to host another 'mystic soirée', but Lord Quayle, in an uncommon show of interest in her activities, thinks it improper to be seen to be hosting *soirées* of any description while their dear daughter is still absent, and I must say that I agree with him. I look at her and wonder how she will swallow the news when it comes to her – whatever the news will be: she looks as if she has not a care in the world as she twitters and waves her hands about. So, she tells me, she must make do with our private consultations. But certainly she would be able, with a little judicious deception, to arrange a quiet meeting for the three of us: herself, myself and Emily, that is. She is most curious indeed to know what this is about. What is this mysterious thing I have seen in the cards? What could Emily have to do with her own fortunes? Is it good news or bad? I tell her I do not know. That I have but seen the signs. We shall unravel the mystery of all these things in due course, I say. She is only to arrange the reading, between the three of us, as soon as she is able. And she must be sworn to secrecy. It was written in the cards – I saw it with my own eyes, deep in the crystal ball.

We must not breathe a word of it, not even to Emily.

*

The next day I receive my friend the footman at the Buttered Bun. He is looking well in his blue suit, but I do not spot him until he is through the door, giving me no chance to escape him and his surly face. Whereas in the yellow he might have been seen a great distance away. But no matter: I enjoy his extravagant scowl and the look he gives me of something that smells very rancid while I read the letter he has brought. It is scented with tuberose, and this is what it says:

My dear Rose,

It is all set. Emily will visit me on Thursday afternoon to take tea. I hope you will be able to join us then. I have mentioned nothing of it to her. She will be surprised!

Until then,

Yours, always

Margaret, Lady Quayle

PS Did you know the poor dear has hurt her arm? Very badly, it seems. But perhaps you will have seen it in the crystal ball. It seems to be her left, so I hope it will not hinder the proceedings.

*

Between the arrival of this letter and Thursday afternoon I suffer an agony of waiting and of nerves, although it is but two days. It surprises me, for I am a steady enough customer by nature, as you will likely have decided for yourself. I sweet-talk my way through every day and trick my living out of other people's pockets, and I do it with a smile on my face, bold as brass, for bold is what it all depends upon.

But now, as I prepare to leave for Cavendish Square, my stomach is full of fluttering things and my head full of questions. How will Emily be when she sees me? Will she suspect we know her secret? Does she suspect it already? How will I reveal it – reveal her bandaged hand? And once I do, what will it prove? I torment myself with this cloud of uncertainties all the way to Oxford Circus and up to Cavendish Square. I ring the bell, almost hoping I will not be heard, that nobody will come and I will have to go away again. But the door swings open after only a minute.

My surly friend the footman greets me with a face I have not seen before: the corners of his mouth twist upward, his eyes shine like marbles. Unnerved as I am already, I stare at him, quite at a loss, before the penny drops: he has evidently seen other people smiling, in a friendly fashion, and is giving it a try for himself. This is the best he can do, and startling it is too.

'Do come in, Miss Rose,' he says greasily. He's never addressed me by my name before: it drops out of his mouth like hot fat. The sound of it makes the back of my neck prickle. Now I wonder what he has to smile about. For a fleeting moment, as I step across the threshold, I feel as if I am walking into a crocodile's lair. He leads me into the hall and motions towards the stairs. 'You are expected,' he says, 'in the usual room.' Do I imagine an ominous note in his voice? Do I see evil cogs working in the back of his head? I shake myself back to my senses. I will not let these fancies carry me away! Am I not, indeed, expected? And have I not a task before me? And may not my very own skin depend upon my success? The footman grimaces at me again as I take the first step: I see him at the corner of my eye, but I don't look at him. I do not want to give him the satisfaction.

By the time I reach the top of the stairs I have collected myself again. I make my way along the hall to Lady Quayle's sitting room. Her voice drifts out into the corridor, punctuated here and there with her tinkling laughter. I pause before knocking at the closed door, my head bent to it to catch the sound of Emily's voice, but Lady Quayle seems to be doing all the talking.

I imagine that hand, wrapped in silk, remember that severed

finger. A little cold draught blows up my back. Then I knock.

I hear Lady Quayle exclaim inside the room. 'Oh!' she says. 'Here she is at last!' Then I hear another voice, which must be Emily's, muttering something I can't quite make out – evidently she asks who Lady Quayle is expecting, for next I hear Lady Quayle, at the other side of the door, say, 'You shall see, my dear!' in a tone that suggests it is Emily's birthday and her cake is coming in. And then the door is flung open, with 'Surprise!' and Emily and I face each other across the room, with Lady Quayle beaming between us.

Emily Budd looks at me, quite blank for several moments, and then her face seems to calcify. I fancy I can see her mind whirling behind it. In those few seconds I see her turning over questions, ticking off the possibilities like the works of a speeding clock: I hear the frantic clicking of beads, the weighing, the measuring: is she here to read our fortunes? Of course she is, how will I refuse. I cannot, which hand will it be, the other, good enough, good enough, does she know, does she know, does she know?

But she only says, 'Good afternoon, Miss Rose. What a pleasant surprise it is to see you again, so soon. I had no idea you were to join us. Are you quite well?'

'I am, thank you kindly,' I tell her. 'And you yourself, Miss Emily, how are you?'

'I am as well as may be expected, thank you,' says she.

'Now then!' coos our good lady, wanting attention. 'Do let's sit down together around the table, for goodness' sake. Miss Rose, you must take off your overcoat, and look as if you have arrived. Will you have some tea?'

'Thank you, my lady, I will.' More tea is called for. I

surrender my coat, we sit down around the table, Lady Quayle's cheeks shining like the lamps at Regent Circus, her hands a-flutter in her lap.

'Have you brought the crystal ball today?' she ventures, after a short pause – delicately, as if it was a guilty secret we were to share with Emily.

'I have not,' I tell her.

'Oh,' she says, a little disappointed. 'Then are we to have cards, perhaps?'

'No indeed, my lady. Today I shall read your palms.'

She seems satisfied enough with that, but I know she would have preferred the crystal ball all the same. Emily sits quite still, a dark little figure in her chair, with her bandaged hand in her lap.

Well, we must begin somewhere, so I ask who is to go first. Emily pipes up all right then. 'After you, Lady Quayle,' she says, and then 'Oh, I must insist! I can see how very excited you are at the prospect.' Lady Quayle demurs a moment, and gives in, without very much of a struggle.

As she is fussing off her gloves, I turn to Emily. Her eyes are two blank black marbles. 'What a marvellous convenience – for the purposes of palm-reading – that it is your left hand, and not the other, that is hurt,' I say. 'I do hope you have recovered a little from your dreadful ordeal.'

'Why, thank you, Miss Rose,' says she. 'Everyone has been so very kind.'

'Well, Miss Emily,' I say, 'perchance we shall find something encouraging in your fortunes to look towards. If you are willing to have your palm read this afternoon, that is? Indeed, I do not believe that we have asked. Perhaps you are reluctant . . .'

'Oh, no,' says she. 'I am quite happy to take part.' She looks straight through me as she says it. Cool as a cucumber. Only her eye gives a little twitch.

Lady Quayle has much the same hand on the end of her arm as she had before. Not many things touch her. There is a half-hearted new set of worry lines, extending across the Venus mount from the base of the thumb, but they fall short of the Vital line somewhere on the way, fading out from lack of interest, things she cannot quite be bothered with. I had overlooked how short her middle finger is – perhaps it has shrunk! It is the finger of family and duty, which stands tall and straight and strong between its brothers on the hands of devoted parents across the wide world, the ones who will lie down in the road before the brewery cart runs over their children's toes. On my dear lady's hand, this Saturn finger is nothing more than a cricket stump, head to head with its neighbours, shirking its responsibilities.

I have to look very hard to find anything new to say that she will want to hear: my thoughts are on the other side of the table, hovering around Miss Emily's bandaged hand. Eventually I tell Lady Quayle that soon she will find something she has lost; that she must be careful with scissors this coming week; and that her heart looks to be in excellent health.

At last, she folds her palm with a sigh, and I turn my eyes on Emily Budd. She fixes me, boldly enough – only a tiny uncertainty flits across the back of her eyeballs – and holds her good hand out, quite steady. As she crosses my palm with a sixpence it seems to wink at me. I take that square little palm and turn it to the light.

Miss Emily Budd has a hand I remember well. I remember

the tapered fingertips, the low-set practical thumbs. I remember the delicate but unbroken Vital line, the straight Cerebral line, the faithful heart, the hard head. And the red point below the Mount of Apollo: passion, it whispers, hidden desires. No stars, still, or feathers, or a square. But most of all I remember that little cross on the Saturnian line, at its end, that grille upon the Mount of Mars, the Cerebral line sloping to the Rascette, where it ends in another little cross that matches the first.

Fearful, violent death.

All there, just the same, clear as print. Not a line upon Miss Emily's hand has changed.

And, quite suddenly, I want to read her left hand, missing its fingers or not. For there must be something about Miss Tabitha there. As I come to my senses, I am staring at that hand, and she shrinks back a little, and says, 'Why, whatever is the matter, Miss Rose?' and Lady Quayle looks up at this, coming a little out of her reverie, and I say to Emily, 'Whatever do you mean?'

'Oh,' she says, 'I only thought . . .'

And before she can utter another word I stand and lean across the table, and before I know what I am doing, I have reached over and seized her injured hand and I am tearing at the bandage.

She pulls away from me, in a panic, and in so doing it comes away altogether just as the door bursts open, as if one thing had triggered the other revealing, in perfect time, Lord Quayle and my smirking friend the footman. 'Caught red-handed, my lord!' he begins, only the words are dying on his lips – and there, at the centre of this scene, is Emily's crumpled and wretched paw, with its ghastly stump. Lord and Lady Quayle and the footman see it all at once. The bluster dies in

Lord Quayle's throat; the footman's pointing hand droops and the smirk falls from his face. Poor Lady Quayle turns a shade of green.

As for me, I have seen worse things before. 'Why, Emily,' I say. 'What a turn-up.'

I turn to Lady Quayle, who has managed not to faint, but holds fast, and I watch as the penny drops.

*

Well, poor Emily is taken from Cavendish Square directly to Great Marlborough Street police station. She says nothing at all. Her premises are searched, and in the little room she occupies above the shop they find a bracelet: three strings of best pearls, fastened with a clasp of diamonds in the shape of a heart. A fine thing, too fine for a shopgirl. Lady Quayle confirms it as belonging to her dear daughter Tabitha. The policeman removes his hat, and tells my poor bewildered lady that he fears her daughter may never come back.

*

Emily denied all knowledge of the bracelet, or how it may have come to be in her possession, my lady tells me. Indeed, she says, it turned her blood quite cold to see how she protested, in despair of her very life: one might so easily have believed her, to see the way she wrung her hands and wept, such dreadful tears.

And with that she wrings her own hands, and cries her own dreadful tears.

Miss Emily Budd was brought to the station for questioning this afternoon, coming direct from 27 Cavendish Square, where she had been visiting Lady Quayle. By the most extraordinary turn of events it has been discovered that the suspect is missing the small finger on her left hand, which is almost certainly the same digit that was posted to the Quayle household with the ransom note sent on the twenty-seventh of July. (The severed digit has been sent for so it can be confirmed as belonging to Miss Budd.)

When asked how she might account for these circumstances she said that perhaps I would like to do it for her. I told her that the obvious conclusion one might draw is that she was the author of the ransom notes, and the architect of Miss Tabitha's kidnap, or at least an accomplice to it. She said that, yes, indeed, it did look likely. I told her also that it would seem that Miss Tabitha must have escaped, or, perhaps, *died* before the first ransom was delivered, else it would have been her finger that was sent to the Quayle residence.

She put her head in her hands at that, and muttered that she only wished Miss Tabitha had escaped or died, and then she cried quietly. I asked her then where Miss Tabitha was, and she answered, 'With him,' but would not expand upon who 'he' might be.

When I told her it was my belief that the victim was in fact dead, and that she herself was facing a charge of murder, as well as kidnap and extortion, she stated again that she knew for certain Miss Tabitha was alive and well, and would not come back because she did not want to. She looked at the floor as she spoke and remained calm.

Why, then, would you suffer your own finger to be cut off? I asked her. 'Tabitha was never kidnapped!' she said. 'She went of her own free will. If we had cut off her finger he would have had to keep her from running to the nearest town and shouting it down. And then, at the end, he would have had to kill her,' she said. '*And I wish he had.*' I told her I doubted any person would volunteer their finger in such a way. She laughed then, and said, 'What is a finger? I have nine more, and I would not have to lift any one of them with five thousand pounds in my pocket and him by my side?'

This is an ingenious explanation but clearly a fabrication, and Miss Emily, in my view, seems quite mad. Finally I asked her where her accomplice and Miss Tabitha might be now. 'Blown away on the wind,' she said. And who is he? 'I will never tell you that,' she said. I asked her why not, when he had left her to take the consequences for both of them, without a care for what became of her. She said nothing to this, but only closed her eyes and hung her head.

Questioning has been suspended. We are holding Miss Budd for the present.

Chapter Eleven

Rose

Come the trial day, and the gallery of the Old Bailey Sessions house is packed with curious faces, for people have heard about the mousy shopgirl, who is charged with the abduction and murder of a lady, no less. Lady Tabitha Quayle, indeed! An innocent creature, devoted to her poor mother, killed for love, it seems. They have heard her throat was slit from ear to ear. No, somebody else asserts, she was most definitely stabbed through the heart – and not for love but the family diamonds. 'I heard,' pipes up another voice, 'she was poisoned . . . garrotted . . . drowned in the bath.'

'You couldn't credit it, could you?' says someone else. 'To look at the accused and believe such a mousy girl could bludgeon somebody to death. Just look at that timid little face!'

'Oh, but you could. Just look into her eyes. Evil, they are, like the devil himself has taken up residence in her soul.'

The judge calls for silence and the first witness is summoned. It is none other than Lady Quayle, mother of the poor victim.

From their very first meeting our good lady had her suspicions concerning the defendant. Nothing she could pinpoint, she tells the court, just a sense that she was in the presence of a wickedness that fair made her skin creep. Lord Chief Justice Calvert asks Lady Quayle, please, to stick to the facts of the case and leave her suspicions out of it. With some difficulty, and several more interjections by his lordship, she manages to give an account of the matter, sticking mostly to the relevant points of the whole terrible affair. To the accompaniment of gasps from the assembly, the lurid details of the package received at the Quayle house are revealed. They hang on her every word as she tells how she had known instantly, as any mother would, that it was not her daughter's finger enclosed therein.

'Who, then, did this digit belong to?' demands our good Lord Chief Justice. The crowd, rapt, turn their heads to her as one. You could have heard a pin drop. Lady Quayle looks up from under her eyelashes at the diminutive figure in the dock, and raises a trembling hand.

'It was Emily Budd's, my lord,' she says, with a sob in her voice, and buries her face in her hanky to cry quietly, with a little heaving of her shoulders.

Well! Miss Emily Budd, of course, is asked to reveal her missing finger to the court, at which there is a rustling and shuffling as everybody cranes their necks still closer. She replies – rather too clever for her own good – that she is not in posses-sion of the missing finger itself but is happy enough to show the court the stump where it used to be. And this she does, defiantly, as if to say, 'There! Prove it was the one in Lady Quayle's handkerchief if you can, now that it is gone!' Of course, the finger is not available for examination by the court, having gone rotten some ten days before and been thrown out with the rest of the rubbish.

There follow two other witnesses for the prosecution, though they hardly need appear, so set are the jury already. For why would a person take off their finger – by accident, as Miss Emily claims – in the jamb of the cellar door and fail to mention such a thing? And even go so far, as Miss Emily has done, to fabricate this story of robbery in the park? And if Miss Tabitha was alive, why would she not come forward to vouch for her friend? It becomes clear to these twelve upstanding men that Miss Tabitha was dead long before the ransom note was written, and that Miss Emily, or her accomplice, has hewn off her own finger to cover the fact. Why else would she be in possession of Miss Tabitha's pearl bracelet? What other explanation could there be for these sorry circumstances?

In the absence of a body they must, however, content themselves with considering only the count of abduction.

They take not a half-hour in retirement to find her guilty.

And so our good Lord Chief Justice Calvert dons his black cap, and in recognition of the extravagant contempt she has shown for the court, he sentences Miss Emily to a month's spell in Newgate, as well as death, with which she might have had an appointment that Friday and been done with. And as she falls to her knees, a general cry goes up in the gallery, a cheering or a wailing, no one seems sure which. Lady Quayle is ushered out, bustling away in a great tangle of taffeta without a backward glance. And Emily Budd is taken down.

'Well,' says Lillie, that night at dinner, 'have you a mind to see Miss Emily drop?'

'I have not,' I tell her.

'I'll wager Miss Tabitha will be there,' she says, tearing the leg from a pheasant. She dips it into the gravy and sinks her teeth in.

'I'll wager she will not,' I tell her.

'A sovereign.'

'I reckon she's dead and buried, my dear.'

'A pound says she ain't.'

*

I do believe I dreamed Miss Lillie Daley before I ever saw her. I was sleeping upon a cold stone step at the end of the Strand on my third night in London Town – a fitful, fevered sleep, like choppy water – and I opened my eyes to find her standing over me. She might have been an angel, or a demon there, with the gas lighting a halo around her curly hair. I lay still on the step for a moment, just looking up at her. 'I dunno what you're doing here,' she said, 'but you'd best move yourself along. This is my spot, little miss.'

I remember I thought it curious that she called me that, for she looked no older than I, although a good deal harder about the face. I remember thinking also that she did not look altogether like the *gadje* girls who came to the camp to have their fortunes read, but rather flashier and prouder. Her clothes looked too bright and nice for her to be sleeping on a step. 'I beg your pardon, Miss,' I said, getting up, 'only I didn't know you were sleeping here too.'

She looked at me then as if I was mad. 'I'm not sleeping here, dear! Like a poor urchin! Goodness, no!' she exclaimed. I felt ashamed then and hung my head a little, so she could not see my burning cheeks. There was a long pause between us while I tried to keep my tears back: it had been such a very hard and friendless day and suddenly they were ready to fall. She shuffled her feet about for a minute or two. Then she said, 'Aren't you a gypsy girl, my dear?'

'I am,' I told her. Then why was I not with my family? I lifted my face up to look at her in the gaslight. 'My family are dead,' I said. She put her head on one side, like a finch looking at a grub; watched a grimy tear run down my cheek.

'Well, you may as well stay with me,' she said.

For certain Lillie Daley is not everybody's cup of tea. She is brusque, indeed, plain rude sometimes, and unsympathetic. She hasn't the heart for acts of charity and she wouldn't tell you if it suddenly came upon her. But she rescued me from the street and she has been my dearest friend since that day.

*

I do not see Lady Quayle for nearly a month. Her letters stop, the footman does not come. I miss her, in a way, as I make my other house calls. I expect she is mourning her daughter, though Lillie sees her once a week and reports that she seems right enough, and coughs up as usual, more generously if anything. I have a nagging feeling my lady has lost her confidence in my talents. After all, I told her Tabitha would be back before the summer was out and now she thinks it will be in a box. To tell the truth, I doubt myself. Perhaps I am losing my touch. Only my dear Lillie keeps faith in me. 'You said she would come back on her own two feet,' she says. 'That's enough for me. The palm never lies, my dear.'

I think that there has to be a first time for everything, but I do not say so. I don't want to make Lillie cross. She is so very certain of me. Perhaps that is why she has never asked me to read her hand.

Chapter Twelve

Rose

The bells of St Sepulchre ring out from the very core of the city, tolling at midnight for tomorrow's dead, marking their last night on God's turning earth, striking grief into the penitent hearts that know, in that moment, even while they crouch in the dank and dark, or press their faces to the cold bars of the condemned hold deep in the black guts of Newgate, that it is green and pleasant somewhere in this world, that flowers grow, and people love, and promises are kept. The dread sound carries through the night air, striking time with the hammer blows of the workmen putting up the scaffold, ringing horror and despair – death itself calling, rolling down Newgate Street, relentless as the tide – *prepare you, for tomorrow you shall die.* Does Miss Emily say her prayers? Or does she sit upon her dirty straw mattress and stick her missing finger up at London Town and all its filthy spawn?

I stand at the end of Skinner Street, across from that fearful black hell-hole, like a squat colossus on cursed ground, deathly quiet – it seems to suck the very light from the air around – and I say a little prayer for her myself, wish it up the bleak walls, through the cracks, to whichever dark corner it will find her crouched in. Then I cross my heart, with silver, and I walk away.

*

Come the morning, the workmen are gone. The gallows stand tall outside the debtors' door, and the street is heaving with a great crowd, bubbling with chatter, shouting, eating, drinking. And I am found among them, in the company of Miss Lillie Daley, who has dressed up for the occasion. She is in a good humour. Perhaps she has woken up so or perhaps she has caught it from the general company: it seems to hang in the air above the mob carousing at the foot of the scaffold, for most of us are criminals, and we will live to see the sun go down again today.

Miss Lillie pops a walnut in her mouth, cracks it like a tiny skull, spits the pieces delicately into her hand. Inside the gates we hear the bells toll, twelve times, as the prisoners are taken into the press yard. For a moment everyone hushes, straining their ears to catch the striking off of chains. Newgate stares down at us; the chatter starts up again. Lillie chews her walnut.

'Is that a brand new hat?' I ask her.

'Yes it is,' says she, pleased as Punch with herself. 'Do you like it?'

I do not know if I like it or not. It is a fair enough question but I cannot find a thing to say on the subject of hats, not in such a place, on such a day as this. I only stare at Miss Lillie, wishing she had not made me come here.

Fearful, violent death. The words form before my dull eyes, as if around the band of her brand new hat. 'Fearful, violent death,' I murmur, as if reading them to myself.

'What's that, my dear?' says Lillie. 'Is something the matter?' And just as I open my mouth to tell her that I feel as though I am falling, and that I do not care about her hat, the debtors' door swings open, with a dead man's groan, and out they come, the walking dead, bound with the ropes they are to swing from.

The crowd falls silent – only a drunken toff can be heard braying into his porter at an upstairs window opposite. And then the babble rises up again as the condemned walk to the platform where Mr William Calcraft – whose father did the job before him, and his before him – is waiting for them, and climb the few steps and stand atop the drop in Jack Ketch's line, with their feet in a neat row. There are seven, all of them men, but for Miss Emily and an old woman dressed in a bridal gown: she laughs and blows kisses until the moment Calcraft puts the black hood over her head.

Emily stands perfectly still at the end of the line as he advances, her eyes flicking around the ocean of faces. Her lips move: perhaps she is praying, perhaps she is whispering – *fearful, violent death*. Then her eyes seem to fix on somebody in the mob, she opens her mouth as if to shout, and struggles to free a hand, but Calcraft is upon her now. He tests the rope with a sharp tug and places the noose around her neck. She stares wildly, gasps, beseeches him to listen to something we can't hear.

I turn to follow Miss Emily's desperate look, rake the hungry crowd – and there, there she is! Quite changed . . . her hair is tied under a scarf; only one fair curl falls down her neck to give her away. Her skin is brown with sun and gold shines in her ears. But it is her demeanour that is most removed from the girl at the Argyll Rooms in the pink satin dress. She is proud and a little hard – even her eyes seem a deeper blue, and not a flicker in them at the spectacle before us. She doesn't flinch, where the girl in the pink satin dress would surely have cried out and covered her eyes. She only holds the arm of her gypsy beau – and what a handsome couple they are, among the throng of potato faces. All this I see in the span of Emily's last gasp for breath, before the hood goes over her head and the cry goes down the street – 'HATS OFF!'

And then the holding of a thousand breaths. Even the toff at the upstairs window is frozen at his seat.

And then, the drop.

Minutes later, after the struggling has ceased, I look around for Miss Tabitha and her gypsy love. But they are gone.

Chapter Thirteen

Tabitha

Something woke me in the dead of night. Whatever is it that wakes you in the dark? Only a feeling, like a shadow passing over the roof. A dread black shape that crosses your eyelids and is gone by the time you wake with a hollow stomach and a half-eaten thought between your teeth, just gone, only just, so you can taste it still. This phantom touched my forehead in the dark and woke me, and I rose and looked from the window out into the field. A grey mist covered the ground, as if the trees were rooted in cloud. Broken limbs reached across, twisting up to the deserted sky. And there, at the edge of the field, stood the silvery outline of a figure, cloaked, indistinct but faced to the wagon, some thirty paces distant. A cold hand ran its fingers up my spine and gripped the back of my neck.

*

Valentin left me again in the morning. I could not help myself. I flung my heaving body down in the field at his feet and I begged him not to treat me so unkindly. He surprised me then.

I expected a slap or a curse, but instead of shaking me away he bent down to me and gently he took my wet face in his hands and he said, 'Patience, my love. I will be back by sundown and after that I shall never leave you again.'

It is true that I did not believe him. I dared not. But he had never spoken to me so sweetly, never called me his love, and it was enough to make me get up and dry my eyes, and tell him I would wait for him. But, then, what else was I to do? For I was his and no good for anything else – he had taken me almost every day since the first time under the willow tree. But for all my hopelessness, and my ruin, I can say, still, that I would do the same over again.

*

I waited – or, rather, I tried to pass the day faster by busying myself, showing really no appearance at all of waiting, though my head was doing nothing but listening to the ticking of the clock inside it. I washed the clothes, every last garment I could find, and tidied camp, rebuilt the fire. I set rabbit traps, picked wild celery and nettles, and I sat upon the steps and picked the stalk from every one, and when all that was done I set to cleaning the wagon: I dusted every inch of it, and polished all the glass and brass, and beat out the rug and the mattress, and swept out every speck of dust. It was in the far corner under the bed that I came upon my jewellery case: the small one I used to use for travelling, the one Emily had persuaded me to take with me. And I remembered what she had said. I could hear her voice, like a ghost in my ear: 'Do not be rash,' she had told me. 'Keep something to remember her by.' To this day I do not know if by *her* she meant my mother or Miss Tabitha Quayle, with her soft, useless hands and her satin dresses. 'At the least, if you should forget her, keep something for a rainy day.'

I did not know at the time what she meant by a rainy day, and I did not think to ask her. But I had felt a little sorry, and I had taken something to remember my mother by. It was a bracelet she had given me on my sixteenth birthday: three rows of pearls, with a diamond clasp, in the shape of a heart. I remember crying with delight as I opened the little blue box, and throwing my arms around her dear neck, and her fastening it around my left wrist, where I wore it every day until the morning that I left her. And as I had looked at it upon the night-stand, I knew I would be very harsh to leave it behind me, that I may as well forget my own dear mother's face, and so I had put it back into the little blue box and taken it with me. And now here was that little box, in my hand. I had forgotten all about it.

It was as I stood up that I caught sight of myself reflected in the mirror that hung over the stove, frowning a little: my hair was tied into a scarf, and my neck was long, my head high and straight upon it. I saw a tanned Romani woman, jutting her proud chin at a lost girl from Cavendish Square, and I stood and stared at her until I could not see any trace of that girl in the pink satin dress, or recognize her face. And I knew that I would never wear pearls and diamonds again, but only keep them for a rainy day, and let them go as easily as breath.

I opened the lid to look at them, hold them in my hand. But the box was empty.

*

When my love came back he was singing. I heard him coming down the road before he rounded the hedgerow. The sun was going down behind him. He slid off the horse's weary back and led it up the field. He stopped at the foot of the painted steps and looked at me. He smiled, and his teeth glittered against the brown of his skin.

'We are free,' he said. Only that. *We are free.*

And the next morning we were packed up and gone.

*

The weeks that followed were the happiest time of my life. We travelled the roads of the south, from the mouth of the mighty Thames to the white cliffs of the coast. We camped by fields of golden wheat, dotted with wild flowers. We caught trout and rabbits and picked blackberries, ate like kings, slept like babies in each other's arms. And in all that time we did not speak to another living soul.

It seems to be but a beautiful dream now, floating somewhere beyond these walls as I lie here in the dark. Only when I reach under my skirts I feel the little button pinned there, that tiny primrose, delicately carved by those hard brown hands. A pretty thing for a pretty lady. And I long to feel those hands on me again, and I know that he is out there in the black night somewhere, that he longs for my kisses and my touch, and that he will come for me one day. He must.

I never asked him about the pearl bracelet. I wondered about it for a short while and then I stopped myself. I knew that whatever he had done with it was the proper thing to do, in our own best interests, and I supposed he had sold it to buy me a wedding ring.

It was the day that we saw Emily hang that I began to suspect what had happened to it.

And later, much later, when the police returned it to me I knew that he had not sold it at all. At first I imagined he had given it to Emily, which wounded me, but then I thought what a poor love token it made, to give another woman's jewellery, and how Valentin, even with his faithless heart, would never have done such a thing. And when Mama told me how she had finally given me up for dead when they had found the bracelet – for it was so seldom I was seen without it – I knew that Valentin had not given it to Emily at all, but rather hidden it in her rooms for the police to find. And his words rang around my head – 'We are free,' he had said.

Mama is delighted to see it on my wrist again. I wear it every day. It gives me hope.

*

I did not know where we were going that day until we saw the spread of London from the top of Herne Hill. It struck cold dread into my belly. I asked him then, 'Are we to come into it?' for I was afraid, and I wished we must not. But he only told me I must trust him, and I recovered myself, and even thought, just then – though it makes me feel foolish, and ashamed to tell it – that perhaps we were come there for my wedding ring.

There was a bright sunny sky over the city that morning. We came down Newgate Street, with the crowd growing thicker around us, the growling of a thousand voices in the distance like the swell of a boiling ocean, a flock of crows swooping and calling above our heads. I wondered what all the commotion was about until I saw it at the end of the street: the great grey shape of that dread house and the scaffold before it. And all at once I knew we were not come for a wedding ring – stupid girl! – but for something dark and dreadful; and my heart leaped into my mouth and I clung to him with shaking hands.

'Why have you brought me here?' I begged, but it seemed he did not hear me with all the shouting and rabble for he said nothing in reply. We swept down the street on the swell of the mob, as if carried by a tidal wave, step by step towards that unholy shadow, and stopped not thirty yards from the platform, off to the side, by the road junction. Still he said nothing, nor looked at me, but he squeezed my hand. I fought my nerves down with every last scrap of my will, remembered my position, to trust, and follow, and be proud.

A little girl went by on the shoulders of her brother: her hat tipped off her bobbing head and down among the feet of the crowd. It looked to be lost and trampled flat, but lo! Some charmed hand caught it and handed it back to her, beaming. On the other side an old woman chewed a brandy ball. In front someone coughed up something black on to their neighbour's foot; somebody punched their companion square in the face. All around there was a swarming horror of people come to watch their fellows die, as if it were the Lord Mayor's Parade. I clung tight to Valentin's hand, looked into the sky over

Newgate's roof, tried to think of the fresh Kent air, the road, the space all around it.

And then the door swung open, and for a moment there was a hush as the prisoners came into view.

Four men and a young boy, no more than seventeen, in a sorry, ragged line, blinking in the sunlight, looking around them with wide, bewildered eyes as if they had just been born, hands tied with the ropes that would go round their necks. Then came an old crone, in a bridal dress, cackling at the crowd and blowing kisses. And last, behind her, a small dark figure, with her head up and her jaw set: she looked only at the platform, and the scaffold, and the hangman waiting there.

It took me a moment to recognize her. In my mind I had buried my old friend. I was looking at a ghost – I had thought that Valentin had killed her, weeks before, in that copse near Southfleet. And in another moment I knew the awful truth: that my love had brought me to that dreadful place to watch Emily die.

The mob had started up again with their clamouring and hooting and cheers. Valentin stared ahead, only breaking his attention away to cuff a young lad who was dancing on his foot. My head swam. What had Emily done? And how did Valentin know of it? And why must we be here? Why must we witness this terrible thing? But I could only watch, as if I was dreaming, as she approached the platform and climbed the steps. At the top she started to mutter something under her breath, a prayer it must have been, for mercy on her poor soul, but her face remained impassive: I could not tear my eyes from it, not even when she began to rake the crowd with that cold gaze and I knew that somehow she would see me there, with Valentin, and I longed to hang my head and hide in the sea of people. The old woman next to her threw flowers and laughed, harder, as the hangman drew down the line, tying nooses around their necks, covering their heads. The boy shook and wept. Emily only flicked her eyes across the crowd, back and forth, and then – and then – they landed on mine. For a moment she stared, piercing me, turning me to stone, though my blood churned through my veins – then every muscle in her body seemed to stiffen, and in the next instant she was looking not at me but at Valentin, with a curious shade across her face, wistful and intent, as if he was the only person in the street. I looked up at him and he was staring back at her, quite still, insensible to the jostling crowd and the boy standing on his foot. I squeezed his arm but he did not seem to notice. He only stood, stock still, eyes locked with Emily's. And all at once that terrible fear gripped me, as it had all those weeks before, that she had stolen a piece of his heart and it consumed me so ravenously that I was glad, suddenly, that she was to die – yes! I was glad! Indeed, I urged it on. If I could have I would have climbed up and pushed her down the drop with my own hands, only so that they would stop looking at each other in that way – rooted to the spot, as if the other were the only soul in the wide world.

Then Emily's face seemed to crack, and she gave a little cry, and raised her hand to point at him. In another moment the hood was over her head and up came a great cheer and a cry, 'HATS OFF!' as if it was a game we were all playing, and the crowd held its breath – indeed, the earth seemed to cease its turning and hang on the edge of the universe – and then the trap at their sorry feet opened with a sound like a gunshot, and down they dropped.

I do not know if Emily struggled. I only heard shouting, and thudding, caught a glimpse of legs kicking, and some of the crowd pulling on the feet of the hanging men, a drooping bridal dress, still as if it were hanging in a closet. I buried my face in Valentin's chest.

We were gone before they cut them down.

Chapter Fourteen

Rose

Emily Budd's swinging legs haunt my dreams. I see her above me, standing upon that dread platform, with her toes at the edge of the trap and then I hear that noise: the step pulling back, like a whip-crack – and down she goes before the howling crowd; ugly faces, a trampled hat, a handsome man, a flash of golden hair. I wake with a start, as I have the last three mornings, nerves a-jangle, and though the policeman is not outside my window, I feel a gnawing in my bones somewhere, as if a worm was carving guilty words through my very marrow.

Fearful, violent death.

What matter Emily Budd's misdemeanours now that she is so very dead? It was I who sent her to the drop. I, and Miss Tabitha Quayle, with her cold blue eyes, like wet stones.

I write a letter to Lady Quayle as soon as I rise. It smells of guilt and foolishness, and this is what it says:

My dear Lady Quayle,

I hope you will find time to receive me this afternoon. I must give you urgent news.

Your servant, Rose

*

'What is this urgent news, my dear?' Lady Quayle asks me.

I wish she would not call me 'my dear'. If she knew what I was to tell her she would certainly not call me that. I take a deep breath.

'I have seen Miss Tabitha, my lady,' I tell her.

She looks at me as if she were waiting still for me to speak. At last she says, 'You must be mistaken, my dear.'

'I am not, Lady Quayle,' I say.

There is another pause, blanker and longer still than the first. 'Is this a cruel trick, Rose?' she demands. 'First I must suffer the loss of my daughter and now, while I am still in black, you bring this fancy to torment me? What is the meaning of it?'

'I swear it, my lady,' I tell her.

'Where? Where have you seen her?'

'At Emily's execution.'

'At Emily's execution? And a week hence you choose to tell me? I do not understand it.'

Now I am not even Rose, let alone 'my dear'. And it has not been a week that I have been wrestling with my conscience, though I do not correct Lady Quayle on that point. For a moment I wish I hadn't told her at all. But then I watch her face cloud over as she starts to follow the thread.

'Emily is dead,' she murmurs first, as if she had only now

realized it. 'Oh, my good Lord, but . . . Emily is dead.' And then, 'What are we to do?' She sets down her shaking teacup and looks up at me, her eyes wider than saucers, like question marks, empty pools in her head. 'You said she would come home,' she says. 'Whatever am I to do, Rose? What am I to do when people see that Tabitha is not dead after all, and Emily is innocent? How am I to live it down?'

'Tabitha is coming home,' I say, 'before the month is out. Only be glad of that, my lady.'

*

My good lady takes some time to decide how glad she is of it – two days, indeed, of fretting and wearing tracks into the carpet, and furrowing her poor brow, which is not used to such a strain. She calls for me, on the second day, to look into the crystal ball.

'Let us say Tabitha returns to us, Rose, what do you see then? How is she to be received?'

With open arms, my lady, surely! She is your own daughter, after all. But of course that is not what she is getting at. 'I am not sure I understand quite what my lady is asking,' I tell her.

She hesitates for a moment, wondering what way round to put it. 'Do you see a great big fuss, Rose? We have our . . . *her* reputation to protect above all . . . do you see problems – in the social way of things, that is . . .'

'Rejection, do you mean, my lady? Humiliation and exclusion from society's circle?'

'Yes!' she cries. 'Exactly so, Rose. Is that what we . . . *she* is to suffer if she returns? For I could not bear to put her through such a trial.'

The crystal ball does not work like that. Indeed, even if I had any talent for crystal gazing it would not work like that. It will only show you pictures of the future. You cannot ask it to suppose this or suppose that, and show you what will happen then, or ask it what you should do. It doesn't care if you turn left or right or marry a lord or fall down a well. It doesn't care about Lady Quayle or her reputation, and it cares even less about her daughter than she does. It is only a ball of crystal, after all.

'Well, my lady, I can look.'

'Yes,' she says. 'Please. Look.'

I see nothing much that helps her, I am afraid. Nothing that addresses her very particular concerns, that is. I see a girl. A lonely girl: Miss Tabitha, with her golden hair tied under a scarf. She sits in the dark – indoors, inside a room? I squint into the ball. No, no, it moves, and shakes, and creaks along the road – a wagon, a gypsy wagon! There she sits, with her head in her hands, crying into the dark.

She must be found, my lady, and brought back.

*

At last Lady Quayle's conscience takes a hold upon her and forces her to the door of her lord's study. She tells him what she knows. He is not happy to hear it. But what else is he to do except call the police and report the kidnapping of his dear daughter, who is not murdered, after all? He offers a reward for her safe return, which is advertised upon bills that are posted across Kent, from Dartford to the south coast. And, this being done, he retires to his office once again to pace, and stare out of the window, and wish that his daughter had been born a son.

Chapter Fifteen

Tabitha

W e saw the bill outside Ashford, not twelve miles from the coast. Indeed, I saw it from a great distance off: a bright white notice tacked to a tree by the roadside, like a flag. And perhaps it is a fanciful notion but I could swear I felt an ominous tremor in my very guts as we approached it, even before we drew alongside the tree and I saw the face upon the bill – a man's face, carefully sketched, with dark eyes and gypsy hair – and read my own name there, in black and white; my own name, in print, which seemed so strange: it seemed to belong to somebody else.

'SHE IS DEAD!' I wanted to shout. 'Miss Tabitha Quayle is a dead thing!'

Valentin was quite still. He only stared at the notice, and then he got down and reached over the hedge and tore it from the tree. When he got back up on the wagon he said nothing.

*

As the sun began to climb down the sky we stopped. I can see the place still, every time I sleep, every time I close my eyes.

There was a stream, and a pair of elm trees, dotted all about their branches with nests. As we drew up the wagon a cloud of rooks took off, wheeling into the air above, calling, circling in angry loops before the setting sun.

Had I known what was to follow I might have heard them crying, *This is where it ends* . . .

Valentin had spoken not a word all the day long. And now he sat with the crumpled bill in his hands upon the painted steps, still he did not ask me to read it. He knew what it said. I let him be and set to, lighting a fire, though there was nothing to cook. I was sweeping away the dust from around it when he came up behind me and took the broom from my hands. He bent his head to me and kissed me, once, long and hard, and then he drew back and looked at me – as if he could see into my very soul. It made me blush and lower my eyes, but he took my face in his hand and turned it up and fixed me there, as though he had nailed me to the tree. He tore me apart with those black eyes. He cut me into tiny ribbons, shaking in the evening breeze. And then he threw the broom down upon the ground and he took my hand and he said, '*Kamauhtut*, Tabitha. Come, now, my lady, my love. Now we jump.'

Do you know what it means?

We took a breath and we jumped together over the broomstick. We seemed to hang in the air like the rooks skating overhead, and the world seemed to shrink and fall away, and when we landed on the other side we were husband and wife. He took a ring from his pocket and put it on my finger. A silver ring, two hands entwined, holding a blood-red stone.

'Never forget me,' he said. I should have known then, but

I was not listening. I only thought of it the next morning when I woke and found he was gone.

*

He left money. A hundred pounds, folded inside a letter. *Forgive me*, it said. *Burn the wagon. Go back.*

In a daze I raked the embers from the fire and set them under the wheels. Then I stoked it and stood back as the wagon burned. I watched the flames lick up the sides, tear through the painted wood, burst from the roof. I know my love would have been proud of me. Then I turned my back and stumbled out to the road, sleepwalking, without looking back.

A passing farmer picked me up by the roadside and took me to Maidstone. I barely remember the journey. When I alighted at London Bridge it looked like a foreign land. Two hackney cabs refused me. The third took me back to Cavendish Square, through streets full of strangers, alien bricks and mortar and railings and traffic and clamour, all a-whirl round my numb head.

And there I was, on my mother's doorstep, my hand stretching out to ring at the bell.

It was the footman who answered the door. He took one glance at me and said, 'Be on your way.' He was closing the door again as I put my hand to it.

'Do you not know me?' I said. He stopped then – it was the sound of my voice that brought him up short for he peered at me for a long moment, through the brown skin and the gypsy gold, and I watched as he saw Miss Tabitha Quayle beneath it all, and his mouth fell open.

'My lady – Miss Tabitha?' he stammered. I only glared at him and passed into the hall. I seemed to hear those rooks cawing and wheeling into the ceiling, high over my spinning head. And then I fell into his arms, and as I went I wished I would never wake again.

*

I suppose I should feel sorry for my poor mother, for all her tears and her wailing, but I could not. I was as a walking corpse in that house. When I came to she had taken the scarf from my head and smoothed out my hair across the pillow.

'Oh, my darling girl,' she said. Over and over again. 'Oh, my dearest girl, my Tabitha, whatever has become of you?' I closed my eyes again and tried not to hear her. I only saw that burning wagon, the broomstick on the ground, Valentin's hands upon the horse's neck, his black eyes.

When I opened them again the doctor was standing over me. I had had a dreadful shock, he told my poor mother. See how blank my eyes were, as if they had nothing better to look at than the wall. And my pulse, a mere twitch in my neck, my blood barely creeping through my veins, my gums pale and wretched to match the inside of my eyelids. I needed rest, and protein, and a special tonic. I heard him prescribe it at my bedside, and at that I turned my head towards the sound of his voice and I begged him for laudanum, to let me be, to let me sleep, I said, though I meant to let me *die*. And then I felt the sharp scratch of a blessed needle inside my elbow and I was gone again, to that meadow by the stream, with the rooks calling and swooping overhead. And written across the sky behind them, in my own hand—

Tell my mother I shall never come back.

Report made this 30th September 1860 by Sgt John Grimes of Maidstone police office

This afternoon another gypsy fellow was brought in for questioning, after a member of the public saw him in town and noted his likeness to the picture on the bill referring to the kidnap of Miss Tabitha Quayle. I saw as little resemblance to it in his face than I had in those of the other three men we have questioned this week. However, he was picked up all alone, which seemed unusual, and I thought I might ask him about the burned wagon found yesterday, on the common ground down by Mr March's lower field, near Romney Marsh. First I asked him his name, which he said was John Thomas. This is likely to be untrue. Next I asked him where he had come from. 'Yesterday?' he said. 'Or the day before? Or the day before that? It is said that a Romani blacksmith made the nails for our Lord's cross,' he told me, 'and so we are doomed to wander the earth for ever. So it would be hard, you see, to tell you where I came from'.

'Yesterday will do,' I told him. 'Just tell me where you were yesterday.'

'Well,' he says, 'I have been following my nose. In fact, the horse has been leading the way. But I have not come far. Eight miles, perhaps, from somewhere near Romney Marsh.' Then I asked him how he could account for his time since yesterday. 'I do not believe I am obliged to account for my time,' he said. Which is true enough. So I asked him if he knew anything about the burned-out wagon by Mr March's lower field, where he said he had come from, and he replied that he had never heard of Mr March's lower field but that he had left his wagon to burn by a stream somewhere near Romney Marsh all right. I asked him why ever he had done such a thing. Did I not know, he asked, that when a Romani passes on, we burn their wagon down with all their worldly goods inside it? I did not know, I told him. Then I asked him who it was that had passed on. 'My wife,' he said. He lowered his head then and seemed quite overcome. I told him I was very sorry indeed for it.

Finally, after giving the fellow some moments to collect himself, I asked him if he knew anything about a Miss Tabitha Quayle. 'I have never heard of such a person,' he said.

I terminated the questioning at that point and let him go. It seems to me he has been as straightforward as a Romani might be expected to be under police questioning, freely volunteering information that he might easily have kept to himself, and that he is clearly suffering the loss of his dear wife. I have no reason to believe he has anything to do with the kidnapping of Miss Tabitha Quayle.

Report made this 30ᵗʰ September 1860 by Sgt R. Duff
of the Great Marlborough St police office

I visited the Quayle household in Cavendish Square this afternoon to interview Miss Tabitha Quayle about her recent abduction. She returned to her family home yesterday under
mysterious circumstances. Her mother told us that she merely
'turned up on the doorstep'. No ransom had been paid, she
said, and Tabitha was unharmed and in good health, though
'dreadfully freckled'.

On arrival at the house, Lady Quayle informed me that her
daughter was resting in bed, but that I might talk to her
upstairs for a few minutes. The victim was quiet when I came
in, and seemed vague, as one would expect from someone who
has suffered such a trauma – when Lady Quayle announced
me she said nothing, regarded me vacantly, then looked away.
I told Lady Quayle that it would be better to talk with Miss
Tabitha alone and she left the room. Can you describe the men
who took you? I asked Miss Quayle to start with. 'They were
tall,' she said, 'tall and burly, two of them. One drove us in
the carriage to Emily's mother's house.' *To* Emily's mother's
house? I asked her, the statement from the now deceased Emily
Budd had stated that the alleged kidnappers had held up the
carriage on the way to the station. Perhaps Emily was right,
she said. It seemed so very long ago now, perhaps she was
mistaken. Emily Budd had had a hand in her kidnap, I told
her. Did she not know? 'No,' she said. That was not possible,
Emily was her dear friend. And what happened next, I asked

her, where did these men take you? 'I do not know,' she said. Did they mistreat you? 'Not especially,' was her reply. And would you know them if you saw them again? 'In an instant,' she said. Then I asked her, how had she come to be at liberty? Had they let her go? Or had she escaped?

She turned to look at the wall, with a curious, sad demeanour. 'They let me go,' she said. That was all she could report. I did not press her further on this question in her delicate state. Finally I told her that I was pleased to see her back in the bosom of her family, safe and well. She looked at me, directly, and said, 'Lady Tabitha Quayle is a dead thing.'

At that point I decided the victim would be better left to rest for the moment, and to pursue my enquiries at a later date.

I spoke to Lady Quayle on my way out, telling her that I would leave any further questioning until her daughter had recovered herself. She has had a dreadful ordeal and exhibits all the symptoms of such a trauma – the confusion, mania and morbid imaginings to say nothing of her changed appearance – and it is unlikely she will be able to tell us anything of use for at least a week, more likely two or three.

She agreed, but added that she hoped Tabitha would be 'up and about in time for Lady Jocelyn's dinner next Friday'.

Chapter Sixteen

Rose

'All she does is look out of the window, Rose. It is all she will do the whole day long. She will not speak, indeed, and barely eats. All she will take is a little soup, and if I find she has risen from her bed it is only to discover her downstairs in the kitchen with Cook. As I open the door she falls silent and looks down into her lap. I am at my wit's end, Rose. I do not know what to do, how to comfort her.' Poor Lady Quayle. Just as she resolves to devote herself to her dear daughter she finds that her daughter is not really there at all.

'May I see her?' I venture.

My lady's face creases as if to cry again. 'Her face is so very brown!' she exclaims, absurd as grieving people can be.

'Let me see her, my lady,' I say.

And so I am led to Miss Tabitha's room. I leave poor Lady Quayle at the door, knowing she will be pressing her ear to it. Inside the room it is dim, the curtains drawn across the windows. Tabitha is but a dead shape on the bed.

I draw near to her and take in the freckled face, the scarf-like shroud across her shoulders, twisted around her sleeping hands, the silver band upon her finger: two hands entwined around a blood-red stone, like a severed heart. She opens her eyes and looks at me. Something in them is hard, very hard. I was going to ask her how she is feeling but I do not. Instead I only stand there, and we look at each other through the gloom, quite still, caught by some invisible line. After a time the corner of her mouth curls into what might be a tiny smile, or a sneer. She lowers her gaze, as if she were going to fall asleep, and whispers something – I have to bend my head to catch it.

'Mother told me,' she says, 'that it was you I had to thank for bringing me home.' Here she flashes her ice-blue stare up at me again, and it makes me start backwards a little, for it is so very piercing and furious. She lifts her head from the pillow and makes a face as though she tasted something bitter. 'Do you know you have finished me, Miss Rose Lee?' she hisses. 'Do you know you have taken my life from me?' I only stare at her, struck dumb. Then she smiles, a curious smile that twists across her face like a curse. Her teeth shine white against the brown of her skin. She lays her head back down into the shadow and puts out her hand, palm up.

'What does it say now?' she asks.

*

'And what did it say?' Lillie asks, over the fish ordinary, at the Three Tuns, Billingsgate – which is cheap, and makes a change. Lately we have let Lady Quayle's charitable activities slip again. 'Is she likely to die, or run away soon, and give us another go at her poor dear mother?'

'Lillie Daley, you shock me more every time you open your pretty mouth,' I tell her. And, really, she does. Or perhaps it is not her who is growing harder about the head but I who am getting altogether too soft. 'I didn't read it,' I say.

'Oh,' says Lillie. 'Why ever not?' She spikes a sprat with her fork, tears off its tail. 'Weren't you curious?'

Indeed I was not. There was something about Miss Tabitha, something like a hex about her. The hurt, and pain, and ruin of the girl, like a proud wild thing trapped – wretched and alone and hostile. And though she had let Emily swing, I wished then that I had left her to roam the wild woods with her gypsy love. And it made me want never to read fortunes again.

I do not say any of this to Miss Lillie, working her way through a plate of flat fish across the table. I shrug as if I do not care about it at all. 'Shall we go on after to Holborn Casino?' I venture instead. 'I've a fancy to get blind drunk.'

*

The next I hear of Miss Tabitha, or indeed any of the Quayle family, is a week later. The surly footman calls upon me again, in the middle of my breakfast, as he always must do. My egg sits congealing on the plate as he hovers over me, sneering gently, drumming his foot upon the floor. The letter smells of rosewater, and this is what it says:

Dear Rose,

Indeed I do not know what it is you said to Tabitha,
but I must thank you for reviving her. After you left last
week she rose from her bed, and asked for a bath, and once
she had taken time to dress her hair, and compose herself
she came downstairs, with not a stitch of those gypsy rags
on her back, but turned out in her best lace dress! She did
not speak much, except to bid me good afternoon, but sat
and took some tea, and a little cold meat. And every day
she seems stronger and more restored to herself. Even the
dreadful freckles lately decorating her face are fading.
Truly I can never thank you enough. You must call one
day soon to see this happy circumstance for yourself.

With all my fondest wishes and gratitude,
Margaret, Lady Quayle

I fold the letter and look at the footman. He crosses his
arms, in the manner of a policeman who must cart me off to
the station for questioning.

'Shoo!' I say, with a little wave to dismiss him. 'Take your
sour face away and leave me to my breakfast.'

*

I do not call at Cavendish Square to witness Miss Tabitha's
happy circumstance. I leave the Quayle women to go about
their business. Lillie asks me if we might resume our caper
with her ladyship, but I have no heart for it. When I look into
the future, along the lines in my own hand, I know that I shall
never see or hear from Lady Quayle again.

*

'You are out of sorts, my girl,' Mrs Bunion pronounces, as she brings me up hot tea. 'Look at you, staring out of the window with your moon eyes. Are you in love? It's a bad bet, you know.'

'Thank you, Mrs Bunion,' I reply. 'No, I am not in love with anyone at all.'

'Who is he?' she says. 'Is he handsome? I'll wager he is, by the look of you. I've never seen such a sulk.'

'Truly, Mrs B, there's no man. You'd be the first to know.'

'Mmm, yes, handsome – and wayward, I'd say. Whispers sweet nonsense in your ear, does he? Calls you pretty names?'

'No, Mrs B.'

'Well, good riddance to him, my dear. Plenty more fish in the sea,' she says, shaking out my blankets. 'Now, I've done well with Mr Bunion, you see, he's a good fellow, stays well out of my way. Always about, but somewhere else. Indeed, I've not seen him for days – I expect he's got stuck in his chair.' She gives me the once-over and pinches my cheek fondly. 'You drink your tea, dear. You'll have forgotten all about him by the time you see the bottom of the cup.'

She has never had children of her own, Mrs Bunion, which is likely a good thing. I expect that she and Mr Bunion have never been long enough in the same room to make any. At any rate, she is much like a mother to me. Once she has gone I drink my tea, as I am told. By the time I see the bottom of the cup I am thinking about my real mother. I lie upon the bed and stare at the ceiling.

I am out of sorts.

*

My own mother, the woman who gave birth to me, ran away with a *gadje* on the morning of my twelfth birthday. I do not remember her face. That is, I remember a face, but I am not sure that it is hers. My father set out after them, with his brothers in tow. They were gone for three days. By the time they came back I was gone, for good. I sent word only to my grandmother, who begged me to come home, but I never replied.

I believe they killed that man. I believe they killed him and dumped him by the Gravesend road. I heard someone speak of it – a stranger, to his neighbour, outside a pub in the Strand – just a week after I had crossed over the river, never to return to the south side. It was them filthy gypsies, they reckoned. Him tied like that, face down in a ditch. Didn't they use that road all day long? Dirty filthy gypsies.

And so I put them out of my mind. I made my own way, my own luck and my own living, and soon enough my mother was a distant, fading wisp of a thing behind me, far away across the water, and all of them but a trace in my memory – as if I had imagined Dulwich, and the common, and that dark circle of wagons and tents, the children running all about, the horses, the black-eyed women.

I dream of her sometimes, coming back behind them, hands bound. They cut her loose by the wagons and put a strap between her teeth and then they flog her. And though she has brought it upon herself I wake in a sweat and for a moment I am twelve years old, on my own on a shop step in the Strand.

Chapter Seventeen

Tabitha

Mother was overjoyed when I cast off my gypsy clothes. And the paler my face grew the happier she became. I sat in the drawing room with her, and made polite conversation with various callers who had come to look at the wayward Miss Tabitha Quayle. I fear I disappointed them: no doubt they were expecting to find me pregnant, or scarred, or full of vile curses. Mama was delighted with me. After they had left she would take my hands and kiss me, and beam at me. 'Tabitha,' she would say, 'you are a good girl!'

She loved me very much, she told me. How happy she was to have me at home again!

But the irony of it was that I was not at home. My body was returned to her, but she did not notice that my head, my heart, my very soul were somewhere else.

It was mid-October and they were over the river, in Dulwich, upon the common where the gypsies camp for the winter.

*

I stole from the house under cover of darkness three long weeks after I had arrived. Mama had retired for the night and everything was still. A sliver of light shone under the door of Father's study, where he had locked himself up every moment that he was not at his club. I stopped and held my breath, strained my ears towards it. I could hear him snoring gently inside. I slipped along the landing and down the stairs, and in another moment I was standing in the street. A toff slowed his pace across the road to have a look at the woman loitering on the steps of number twenty-seven. We stared at each other in the gaslight before he cursed under his breath and spat at his feet, moving on again. The Dog Star broke through the cloudy sky ahead as I crossed Cavendish Square, heading south, for the river.

No hansom cab would take me until I reached Charing Cross and even then I was obliged to ask several before I found a driver willing to go to Dulwich Common. We drove down Whitehall, past Westminster Abbey and south along the river, into territory unknown to me. The air seemed to grow heavy and damp, a little rancid. The opposite bank of the river appeared, a jagged line of mean little dwellings: a tangle of beams and sheets of tin glowing in the moonlight, yellow lamps burning here and there behind greasy windows. A great grim building loomed up on our right, making me start. I opened the trap at my head. 'What is that place?' I asked the driver.

'That's Millbank Prison, miss,' said he. 'The largest in London. It's from Millbank they ship 'em out to Australia. Now, that's a fate worse than death, if you ask me.'

'Quite so,' said I, watching the towers of it pass over my head and fade into the dark as we crossed Vauxhall Bridge.

I had never been on the south bank of the Thames before.

*

The way grew darker as we went deeper south. We clattered past black fields, little rows of cottages, railway bridges. I recognized Herne Hill as we went past it. Large country houses loomed at a distance back from the road, a public house here and there lit up the night. Then great stretches of gloom before the next one, all ablaze with gaslight on the corner. And then just the road again, rolling out before us. At last we came to a stop, under a street lamp. The road was deserted: not a sound came from the sleeping houses nearby.

Over the way lay a great open dark space. It might have been a plain, or a lake, for all I could tell. A gentle wind blew over it: the smell of fresh air and a tang of camp fire.

'Where is this?' I asked the driver.

'This is where you get down, miss,' he said. 'The camp's just over the way there.' He pointed to a dark line of trees and, just visible, crouched beneath them, a wide group of wagons and tents, spreading across the field. 'I'm sorry, miss, but I'll not take you any closer than this.'

'Would you wait for me to go back, please?' I said. He laughed at that and shook his head. I pleaded with him, for I was afraid to be left there for the night, and then he relented, and told me he would wait for no more than a half-hour, and that I must pay for the journey out, and the waiting, now. And that if he saw me coming back with anyone else he'd have to leave me there. 'Very well,' I told him, and paid up the money.

And then I was standing at the edge of the Romanis' field, with the moon overhead and the breeze ruffling the grass at my feet, and my hot heart beating in my mouth.

It was a daunting thing, to approach that camp. As I came nearer I could hear children running in and out of the circle, fires crackling, the murmur of voices. I was glad that I had not stopped to think about coming more thoroughly, because I would have seen that it was a foolish thing to do, and might not have come at all. Who was I to speak to? And what would I say? How should I announce myself? My hope that Valentin would be among them suddenly seemed a fragile thing . . . and if he was, might I find him with another woman? I would kill myself if that were so – indeed, the very thought of it made me feel dizzy, and sick with fear: as if I would drown in the middle of that open black field.

I was obliged to stop and compose myself, try to bring my shaking nerves under control, but still my head whirled with possibilities. Might he be angry to see me, rather than glad? Perhaps the Roma would disapprove of a *gadje* setting foot in their camp at this late hour, and what if his family shunned me? Could that be why he had never taken me to them, month after month, when he had said we would catch them up in Rush Green, and Kent, work at pea-picking, and hopping, and the fruit harvest? Why had we never gone after them to those places, to be with the others? Did he not love me? Was he betrothed to someone else – was he ashamed of me? All these things spiralled around my skull, like a cloud of midges in the night air, as I reached the camp, rounded the wagons and stood before the nearest fire.

The first creature to greet me was a furious dog, which hurled itself forward to the end of its chain where it lunged and barked at me until a rough voice called it back. Its swarthy Romani master came forward, glowering at me in the light of the fire. 'What are you after, lady?' he said. One by one Romani faces appeared, glowing golden brown, watching, with dark shining eyes.

'I am Tabitha Quayle,' I said. My voice sounded thin on the chill air. 'I have come to look for my love.' And all of a sudden I realized that I knew Valentin only by his first name, and no other, and felt more foolish than I had before. But I had gone too far to turn back. And I did not care.

'His name is Valentin,' I told them. 'And he is one of you.'

Chapter Eighteen

Rose

'His name is George Dent,' whispers Lillie into my ear across the tablecloth. 'He's the twelfth Earl of Leland.' She sits back, beaming. 'He's rich, all right. And he's a proper poppet to boot. And handsome? Oh! I should say so!'

I am sure I have heard that name before somewhere. George Dent. I don't remember where. Anyhow, Lillie certainly seems taken with him. She is in fine form, which I am not, for some reason. Indeed, I am having trouble making conversation, of the sparkling dinner variety anyway.

'Make sure he treats you like a lady,' is the terrible banality that trips off my tongue before I can stop it – though I do mean it and it is good enough advice at that. Lillie looks at me hard, most likely wishing she had gone to dinner with somebody else.

'What's up with you?' she demands. I push my chop around my plate, wondering where to begin. I can feel her opening her mouth to tell me to spit out whatever it is and be done with it. I take a deep breath. I have not spoken any of it out loud.

'I have been thinking about my family,' I tell her.

She says nothing, but only swallows her steak down with a fresh glass of sham.

'About my mother,' I add.

'What about her?' she says.

'Well,' I tell her. 'I have been wondering if they still stop on Dulwich Common for the winter.'

'Who knows indeed?' she says then. She looks at her plate, her knife and fork limp in her hands, as if she is suddenly full, and looks back up at me. 'Whatever has brought this on?' she asks, as if she doesn't much want to know the answer.

Lillie and I never talk about the past, but only look forward. And now that we turn to look back it is an uncomfortable thing. She doesn't say much, only that she cannot see the reason in digging up old bones. She does not tell me it has been twelve long years and that my home and all my friends are here – or remind me of how very lost and wretched I was when she found me, or how cold it was on that shop step, or that my own mother did not love me. She doesn't think I should go to Dulwich. Why should I want to? She says they don't deserve to see me again.

'Are you worried that I won't come back?' I ask her.

She looks straight at me then, with her bold green eyes. 'Yes, I am,' she says.

*

194

I do not exactly decide, it is more as if I am compelled to go: as if something across the river is calling me. It has been creeping like mist over the water and across the city to Soho Square where it hangs outside my window and taps at the glass, and whispers through the sash every night this last week, and it wakes me, or penetrates my dreams, with cold pointed fingers, and I cannot stand it any longer.

Tonight I shall take a carriage there and I will lay this spectre to rest.

And so it is fixed. And once I have surrendered, that voice relents, and there is peace for a short time, before other devils start to dance around inside my head.

I wonder what I shall find. I wonder all day, as I try to go about my business, what I shall find there and it paralyses me every time I think of it. Can they be there still? Is old Hannah Smith long dead and buried? I am certain the camp will be there, as it is every autumn, for Romani are creatures of habit and tradition – and then, being sure that this is so, I find myself wishing that I would be wrong, that I would fetch up to find an empty field, or a group of strange faces – but in its turn this thought chills my bones and hollows my heart. If I was out of sorts yesterday truly I do not know where I should put myself today. I pace, and sit, and stand again, as if I were trying the stuffing of every chair in the house. And what am I to say to her, or any of them? What am I to say if I find them there? What is it that I want? What if they do not know me? What if they do not welcome me? Only – I know that if I find them they will welcome me with open arms. I am one of their own. They will bring me in and fold me into their circle and I will have to explain why I have never been back. I am frightened that I will find I have been wrong all this time, that I have been in the wrong place. I am frightened that I will wish I had never left them.

*

I take a hansom cab as the dark is coming down. We drive down Dean Street, Princes Street, Coventry Street: I sink into the dark back of the carriage and draw my shawl around me, watch the coloured swirl fly past. It looks like a bright dream, like something I might half remember upon waking and be unable to catch. Laughter and chatter roll by the window as we drive down the Haymarket, all tangled together in a great buzzing ball of noise; it makes my head spin. I look out as we pass the theatre and there is Lillie, at the centre of this riot. She seems, in a new dress of yellow satin, bright like the yolk of an egg. She is looking at a young fellow on the step below her, looking him up and down as he offers his poor red rose. She doesn't see me. I have a sudden urge to call out to her: I have leaned forward in my seat and put my head out. 'LILLIE!' I shout – but my voice falls short in the general racket. She doesn't hear me, and then we have rolled past her and away, and I am craning my neck to see a parting glimpse of her but I catch only a flash of yellow.

And suddenly we are at Charing Cross, turning down Whitehall, and I can smell the river.

I knew I should have to cross it, of course. I have dreamed of crossing it, and woken with a start, in a sweat, terror gripping my belly, then quieted the horrors in my foolish head with commonsense. There is nothing to fear crossing the river, thus, tucked up inside this carriage. But still I see that tiny star flash before my mind's eye: the one on my right palm, on the Mount of the Moon. I shut my eyes tight as we turn left on to Westminster Bridge and all the way across – I seem to hear the water moving underneath us, below the horns and whistles of the river traffic. I swear I feel it sliding under the bridge, like a great grey serpent, and my stomach knots itself into a tight ball and my hands too, until at last we are on the other side. I breathe again, release my fists, laugh a little at myself.

We rattle down streets of plain little houses, workmen's dwellings, rows of trees, a pub. The buildings thin out between the villages, and we are driving by empty black stretches of countryside, still and ominous, trees looming out of the dark and flashing past, falling behind us before another line of cottages springs up in front, a row of shops, another shining pub. I do not know them, or the way. I am quite lost, and it is not long before I am consumed again by fearful things. This carriage is taking me to Dulwich, back to my family, to be served whatever Fate has in store for me there.

Chapter Nineteen

Tabitha

They did not speak for the longest time. They only sat and looked at me in their big ragged circle, and I seemed to shrink inside my clothes, withering under their blank, dark stares. But I stood, defiantly enough, and I kept my head up. Somebody broke away and ran to another fire across the camp. After a while there were footsteps coming back, and there was muttering, and someone pushed through from the back and came to have a closer look at me. She was about my age, and about my height, and she had Valentin's hard brown eyes. She circled me, taking me in from head to foot and back again. Then she stopped before me.

'Valentin told me you were plain,' she said. 'Plain Emily.' She reached up and tore the scarf from my hair. Golden curls fell around my shoulders. 'A *gadje* girl with plain brown hair. But he loved her, so he said.' Everyone laughed at that.

I felt my face burn with shame. 'I am not Emily!' I told her.

'Well, I can see that for myself,' said she. 'Our Valentin has been an unfaithful boy.'

'Is he here?' My poor desperate heart thumped at my breast as I asked her. She had Valentin's dark lashes, his insolent mouth.

She took a lock of my hair between her fingers. 'Is he here?' she said. 'His likeness is decorating bills across the county!' She leaned in, it struck me then, as though to kiss me. 'He is gone, pretty miss,' she hissed, flashing gold teeth. I felt as though she had struck me a blow to the stomach. I could not breathe, and for a moment I thought I would sink to the ground. I tried to beat back the tears that forced themselves from my eyes and slid down my hot face. There was silence all around me. Then, as if she meant to be kind, but mocking me, she said, 'Did he say he would marry you? You're not the first!'

'He did,' I told her. I jutted out my chin and told her to her face. 'Yes, he did!' I said. 'And then he threw down the broomstick and we jumped it.'

Night birds called from the dark trees, the fire spat. Nobody moved, or spoke, but only looked at me, and it made me reckless. I leaned in to her, just an inch, as the condemned might stretch their necks across the block and smile at the axeman as if they cared for nothing. And I held up my hand for her to see the ring on my finger: the two hands entwined, the red stone flashing in the firelight.

'Put that in your pipe and smoke it, gypsy lady,' I said.

I thought she might knock me to the ground. But she only looked awhile, and then she arched her eyebrow, and looked some more, and then she laughed, and said, 'Well! You had better sit down by the fire, my little sister, and have a drink.' And when I looked, a space had cleared for me in the circle.

I knew, even then, what a rare thing it was. She took scissors to the cord that tied me to my mother and my father, my name, my birth, the very fibre of my body, my flesh and my blood and my bones. I sat down into the shadow. Somebody passed me a cup.

Rose

They are only dark shapes beyond the trees from where the cab leaves me. I pay him an extra crown and ask him to wait for me, twenty minutes. As I approach across the fields I hear voices, children, an axe splitting wood. The fires throw orange light, here and there, figures move about before them, sit and smoke, eat, talk. My heart begins to thump, not faster but harder with every step, like a warning: it seems to shrink back into my chest as if it were trying to drag me back up the field, away. And then I am standing next to a wagon, just the other side from the voices and laughter and crackling fire. I can't wait here for long: someone will come round for something and then they will spot me and think I have come to rob them. I must present myself or creep away, like a coward.

I step out from the shadows, around the wagon and forward into the light of the fire. I stand until every face around it falls silent and looks at me. An old man at my left hand takes his pipe from his mouth and taps it on the sole of his boot.

'Good evening, miss,' he says. 'This is an awful late hour to be out on the common.'

'Good evening, sir,' I reply. 'Happen it is. I am looking to have my fortune told.'

'Well!' he says, looking me up and down. 'You might have come in the day with all the others.'

'Only I am looking for one Hannah Smith,' I tell him. 'I have heard she is the very best of all.'

The fire snaps; an owl calls in the wood beyond. The man stands, nods, and I go after him, with all the eyes around the fire following us, across the clearing at the centre of the camp, towards a little wagon parked inside the circle of the others.

As we draw near I see it clearer: it faces away from us so that I cannot see the door but only the back and side of it. A yellow light burns in the window behind a lace curtain. When we stop some twenty feet from it, I know it. I remember her taking delivery of this wagon, the first in our camp, shiny as a new pin, everybody gathering to see it, climbing the little steps to look inside, admiring the paintwork. The scrolling picked out in gold around the door looks as spick and span as it did that day.

It is my grandmother's wagon.

'Stay here,' he says. I wait in the dark as he goes to it, and up the painted steps, and disappears from view. I count out the time for him to take knocking, and talking, and my heart starts to bang in my chest again. I wait, standing all alone on the open grass with the misty rain starting to dust my face. I look around, behind me, left and right. At the edge of the trees a dark figure watches me. A girl: her face is in shadow – I fancy she puts a curse on me. When I blink she disappears.

And then the old man is there again, at the bottom of the stairs. He comes a little towards me across the black grass and beckons. Then he motions for me to go up.

There are only seven steps but it is a long climb.

The door stands a little open at the top. It's dark inside, but for a small lamp burning orange on the tabletop, lighting a circle of patterned lace cloth that wavers gently as I stand upon the threshold, upon the very edge of the wide world. My breath flutters in my chest, like a trapped winged thing. The old lady at the table moves, and though her face is in shadow I know my grandmother by the way she tilts her head on one side to look at me, and the cards she holds in her left hand.

'Come in,' she says. 'Don't be shy.'

I step through the doorway and into my own lost heart. There is a scent of beeswax, and tobacco, and laundry soap that folds the years of my life back upon themselves and away to nothing, like the creases of a fan.

'I knew you would come,' she says. I've heard her say it before. She used to say it to everyone who came to have their fortune told. I sit down across from her and she looks me in the eye. Her face is old, lined and brown as a walnut; her eyes are holes in space. The merest twinkle flits across the black back of those dark orbs, like a star winking. Does she know me? I take a silver crown from my pocket and hold it up to the lamplight. It flashes in time with the coins in her white hair, the cut glass sparkling on the shelf, the candle above the burner. I reach my hand across the tabletop and cross her palm.

Without taking her eyes from mine she sets the crown upon the table. Then she folds my open hand and pushes it back. She takes up the cards again and puts them into my hands.

I shuffle, hand them back to her, and she lays out the spread. At the centre, the Queen of Diamonds, to represent me. Then she deals them into four piles around it, face down – what is in her mind, what does she step on, what is in front, what is behind? When she has dealt the last card she looks at me for several moments, taking me in, quite still. Just as I am about to ask her, 'Do you know me?' – or perhaps she is about to say that of course she does, it has been only twelve years, after all – she turns the first pile of cards and lays them out in a row.

The Ace of Spades is there, of course: the foundation of my life, my family, has been on my mind for certain. Two Queens, my mother and grandmother. But also meaning trouble, or argument. In the second pile, the things I step on, a black ten, a red seven, two Jacks: nothing I can make much sense of.

Then we come to the third pile. 'Now,' says she, 'we come to what is ahead.' She has her hand upon the pile of cards, ready to turn them, when she stops again, and looks at me, quite intent. I know what she is going to say.

'Life is like streaky bacon, my dear,' she tells me. 'You must remember that. There is fat, and there is lean, and if you want to know the future you had better take them together.' And with that she turns the pile and spreads them with her gnarled hands – and lo! There upon the white cloth are a pair of black sevens and two black tens.

'Death? Whose?' I ask her, though I am not supposed to know the cards. She points to the other two in the pile: a red ten, and the Queen of Spades.

'These tens,' she says, 'are for travel. And the Queen, a fair-haired woman. She is connected to this death, although she doesn't know it yet. Perhaps it is her death, and will affect you sorely. And it is mixed up in some way with a journey. Not a long one but a short journey, to another part of the city.' She looks up from the spread and leans a little across the cloth. 'Perhaps you would be better not to make this journey, my dear,' she says. 'Stay with us, here, tonight. We always have a home for a Romani girl.'

Tabitha

When I saw Miss Rose Lee across the fire I fancied I was
dreaming it. I screwed up my eyes and all but rubbed at them,
but when I opened them again there she was. She spoke to an
old man, I could not hear what they said. She looked all about
her, around the circle, into the shadow, and though she looked
straight through me, she did not notice me. The old man led
her away, across the dark, slick grass. I watched them until
they were pinpricks in the gloom, and then I set down my cup
and made my farewells. They watched me until I was out of
sight around the wagons, and two boys and a dog saw me even
a little further up the hill. Once they had gone back to the fire,
I started around the camp, to the side I had seen Miss Rose
headed, by the trees.

A knot was tightening in my stomach. Was she come here
to see Valentin? The thought of it tore at my heart suddenly,
like a madness, though I had never seen them together or
knew if they had ever met. Could he be here, after all? It
gripped me like a fury as I ran through the dark, and then I
was in the shelter of the trees, coming from behind the camp.
I crouched by a tree near the wagons. All was quiet and dark,
but for an orange glow from a little old wagon at the centre,
and the moonlight upon the clearing where she stood: alone,
looking towards the orange light. I moved forward, beside the
tree at the very edge. She looked about her into the dark. I
knew she saw me, but still did not know me. And then the
man came out of the old wagon and beckoned her in.

He sat upon the bottom step as the door closed, and lit his
pipe.

A dog barked in the distance then, and there was the thud of a stick and a shout. I shrank back through the trees, and ran.

The driver asked me if something had happened as he let me into the carriage, if everything was quite all right. Yes, it was, thank you, I told him, no nothing has happened, I was only rushing in case he would be gone. I needn't have worried on that account, he told me. He would have waited all night rather than leave me here in the dark with these gypsy folk. To tell me the truth, he had begun to worry a little, and would certainly have come looking in another minute or two; indeed, he hadn't felt altogether right letting me go in the first place. I listened, and told him thank you, and wished he would stop talking so that I might have quiet for my bursting head. But he did not. As we set off he was obliged to open the hatch to shout through it, and still he kept thinking of more things to say. His grandmother's second child had been carried off by gypsies and was never seen again, he told me. Well, she never recovered, took herself off to the coast and threw herself into the sea, clean off the top of Beachy Head! And would you believe it but not a week later they found the baby in a camp near Gravesend. They'd put some sort of wretched curse on it, it didn't look the same, didn't look right at all. Well, they left it there, after all, its poor mother was dead . . .

As the journey wore on it became plain that he simply would not desist. I leaned against the window to cool my burning face.

It was Rose who brought me back.

I knew it for she had seen us at Newgate. I knew it was her doing from the moment I saw the dread white paper nailed to that tree. I remembered the look on Valentin's face as he took it down, and I knew it was over. And since that day I had been as good as dead.

Had I heard about the new underground railway that was to run across the city? the driver asked me, shouting so abruptly through the hatch that I jumped. My heart started to bang again against my ribs, and a curious rushing filled my ears. 'A railway under the ground!' he bellowed. 'Whatever next?' No, I told him, I had not heard of it. Digging up North London they were, he said, and making a devil of a mess of it. He'd never seen the like. Had I not heard? No, I said, my voice sounding faint. I had not heard. And all of a sudden I felt as if I was suffocating and I should die if I did not get down and I shouted back through the hatch, 'Stop the carriage! Stop! Stop, at once!'

'Are you quite all right, miss?' he asked.

'No,' I said. 'No, I am not. I must get out. Please, do not fuss at me or ask me anything.'

He pulled the horse up by the side of the road. I paid him and got down. 'I don't like to leave you here all alone, miss,' he said. 'Are you sure you are quite well?'

'I am perfectly well,' I told him, 'but for a throbbing head-ache.' I only wanted to walk a little while, and have some quiet, and fresh air. Besides, we were almost at the river, I would be able to take another carriage there. He drove off into the dark without a backward glance.

I stood still for several minutes, on a little grass verge by the milestone. A light glowed from an upstairs room across the way. Something trampled through the hedgerow. I breathed the night air deep into my chest: I felt as though I was under water, as if I were seeing and hearing everything through glass. And the only things sharp and clear were the pain of being parted from Valentin, the wondering if I would ever see him again. And the hatred, like a cold knife in my heart. It was Miss Rose Lee who had brought me to this. It was she who had torn us apart. Like a blind thing, I stumbled from the kerb and headed towards the river.

I do not know how long it took me to reach the bridge. I walked in a stupor. I remember nothing of it until I saw the water, grey and turgid, catching sparkles of light from the moon. I stopped halfway across and looked down into it, and as I watched it sliding beneath me, I thought I would throw myself down into its depths, let it take me along. How easy it would be. I pictured myself, my skirts billowing out around me, soaking up the river, sinking, dragging me down; the short struggle, my last breath, the blessed peace. I laid my head on the cold rail and dreamed of Valentin, his dark eyes, his mouth, his strong hands. Then I stood up and pulled myself on to the edge of the rail, swung my legs over so that my feet dangled above the water. I said a prayer, took a deep breath and started to count.

Rose

As we drive away from the common I look back to see a group of dark figures watching, sparks flying into the sky behind them. Once they are gone from view, I lean back in the seat and stare out at the trees going by. A row of houses flashes past; a church, a stableyard fly by us, we are making good time. I close my eyes and see the cards laid out upon the table, Hannah Smith's gnarled hands, like the roots of an old oak tree. As I took my leave of her she caught my arm and looked at me, deep into my head for a long while, as though she was reading my mind. Then she said, 'Do not forget me, dear. I shall be here until the spring comes.'

Then she leaned in a little closer as though she was going to kiss me goodbye but she only looked at me, harder still, with the merest frown troubling her old face – as if she was peering at something in the distance – and she said, *Stop for nothing*.

A wind is whisking up the trees outside now, thrashing branches against the black sky. They might be beating me back from where I came. I want to ask her about my mother. I want to pack up my Soho life and leave it behind, bid goodbye to my dear Mrs Bunion and the regulars, to my beloved Lillie Daley, to bricks and mortar and the bright lights of Piccadilly. I want to join my Romani family and live on the road once more.

And then, all of a sudden, we are at Vauxhall Bridge. Before my nerves have a chance to pull tight at the sight of the river churning below, we are upon it, and I do not shut my eyes or clench my fists but instead I look out eastward across the city at the galaxy of lights, spread out over the land as if the stars had fallen down.

Then I see her, perched upon the edge. A dark figure, in

plain dress, she has her legs over the side of the bridge and her head bowed, looking down into the water. I fling open the hatch and shout, 'STOP!'

'Not likely, miss!' says the driver, slowing a little all the same. 'I've seen this before. It's a trick. We stop to help her and her mob will be off with the horse and carriage, and likely our money too.'

'Stop here!' I cry, still louder, furious. 'Set me down at once!'

'Very well, miss. It's your funeral,' he says, and pulls up the horse. He lets me out at the far end of the bridge, as quick as he can, fairly dumping me in a heap on the ground, and then he cracks his whip at the road ahead, and is gone.

The woman is there, still, a dark shape perched at the top of the rail, some way distant. I can see her face turned towards me in the light of the moon. We do not move but only stare at each other. Then she turns her head to look back down at the river.

I find myself running towards her as the bridge stretches into miles of grey flagstone before my feet and I seem to shrink to a tiny gasping speck in the dark, feeling I shall never reach her. And then I am twenty yards from her and she is kneeling up upon the rail and I shout – 'WAIT!' – and fling myself at her and catch her legs and we fall into a tangled heap on the stones. I lie still, recover my breath and my pounding heart, wondering if I have broken something or if I have killed her. When I glance up she is looking down at me. I do not know her for the first moment, and then I see her. It is Miss Tabitha Quayle.

'Why, Miss Rose Lee,' she says, with a strange smile. 'Fancy meeting like this.'

It is as she says it that I hear those words again.

Stop for nothing.

And an ugly sensation creeps over me, with her eyes upon me, like the wicked wolf's. I sit up quickly and struggle to my feet but she is up before me. She seems to tower above me and suddenly I can hear the river writhing below us and my heart leaps into my mouth. And I notice I am standing with my back to the rail. Before I can run she has grabbed me by the neck and she is pushing me over it, and I fight, but my strength is gone and my balance with it and the night sky seems to swell and swallow us, and then I am falling, backwards, down into thick, icy water with my grandmother's warning ringing in my head, and before my eyes my own hand stretched out upon a tabletop, under the lamplight – with that little star, upon it, on the Mount of the Moon – and I know what comes next.

Tabitha

I had counted to nine when the carriage rattled on to the bridge. In just another moment I would have been down in the water, and everything would have been quite different.

The noise of the wheels clattering across the cobbles startled me. I thought I would wait until they had passed. But then I heard a shout – 'Stop!' – and I turned to look and there in the cab was none other than Miss Rose Lee. She had her face turned up to the driver and I caught a flash of it in the moonlight. And then the carriage stopped, at the end of the bridge, and she got down and the driver sped away, leaving the two of us all alone.

I do not think she can have known that it was I perched there above the churning water. She stood some way distant and I could not see her face clearly. And for what reason would she expect me to be sitting upon the rail of Vauxhall Bridge in the middle of the night? No, she had stopped to save me, whoever she thought I might be. And so, I thought I would let her.

I cannot say at what moment I decided I would kill her, or even if I thought of it at all. When I think back on it now it seems a fixed thing, something that was always inside my mind, like printed verses in the book of my life. I looked back down into the water and I heard her shout and her footsteps, running towards me, and I knelt up on the rail and in another second she had grabbed me around the waist and pulled me down on top of her on to the paving stones. When she looked up at me she seemed to see right through me, and then I saw the horror crawl across her face as she recognized who the poor soul was whom she had saved. She scrambled to her feet and her eyes did a little dance of confusion as she tried to read my face. And then my hands were at her throat and – well! It was the easiest thing in the world to push her over the edge.

I watched her drown. It was just as if I was watching the scenario I had pictured minutes before, only it was *her* skirts filling with water, dragging her down, *her* struggle, *her* last breath, *her* death. She disappeared under the bridge and I ran to the other side. When she came out she was still. A dead shape, floating just under the surface, dark hair streaming behind her.

Chapter Twenty

Tabitha

They pulled her out of the river at Wapping-stairs. I have not shed a single tear for her, nor suffered so much as a grain of remorse or regret. My mother asked me, had I heard the news, and twittered about what a pity it was. But then, she said, she expected that a great many gypsy girls must come to a sticky end. And then she carried on with her usual chatter – the society gossip and her latest interest – she has taken up découpage: what a stupid thing! Privately I think she is going quite mad. Today she told me that George Dent, 12th Earl of Leland – whom she was good enough to remind me I had so foolishly rejected back in June, why, she still could not understand. Oh! If only I had not all this would never have happened! – was engaged to be married to one Annie Atkins, currently going by the name of Miss Lillie Daley: a strumpet she claims to have saved from the gutter herself! She had seen them out together at Baroness Chorley's ball. What an outrage, she said. Whatever was the world coming to? I do not hear most of what she says, and I do not care about any of it. I only want to sit in the dark and dream of my Valentin, my love. I do not wear my wedding ring but I am still his wife. I have removed it because it keeps my mother quiet – on that subject at least – and I cannot bear to hear her speak of him. She has not asked me but I can see she knows that he has taken me and that I am spoiled for another man. Sometimes she sits and cries into her paper-paste and I know that is what she is thinking of. If my father knew he would surely disown me: sometimes I am tempted to knock upon his study door and tell him everything – but that would be reckless, and reckless-ness will get me nowhere.

And so I must go through the motions of life at Cavendish Square – I make house calls, and receive visitors, look in shop windows, buy trinkets; and when all that is done I sit here in the drawing room and gaze out of the window, making little noises as if I were listening to Mama, waiting: pretending I am Miss Tabitha Quayle, until the time comes.

Acknowledgements

Many heartfelt thanks to Juliet Brooke, Clara Farmer, Iree Pugh, Parisa Ebrahimi, Hazel Orme and everyone else involved at Chatto & Windus – also to Vivienne Schuster and Felicity Blunt at Curtis Brown.